BREAKOUT FROM STALINGRAD

Further Titles by Leo Kessler from Severn House

The S.S. Wotan Series

ASSAULT ON BAGHDAD
BREAKOUT FROM STALINGRAD
FLIGHT FROM BERLIN
FLIGHT FROM MOSCOW
FIRE OVER SERBIA
OPERATION LONG JUMP
S.S. ATTACKS

THE HITLER WEREWOLF MURDERS

Writing as Duncan Harding

ATTACK NEW YORK!
COME HELL OR HIGHWATER!
THE TOBRUK RESCUE

Writing as Charles Whiting

The Common Smith VC Series

THE BALTIC RUN
IN TURKISH WATERS
PASSAGE TO PETROGRAD

PATHS OF DEATH AND GLORY
(*Non-Fiction*)

Writing as John Kerrigan

The O'Sullivans of the SAS Series

KILL ROMMEL

BREAKOUT FROM STALINGRAD

An SS Wotan Adventure

Leo Kessler

This first world edition published in Great Britain 1995 by
SEVERN HOUSE PUBLISHERS LTD of
9–15 High Street, Sutton, Surrey SM1 1DF.
First published in the USA 1995 by
SEVERN HOUSE PUBLISHERS INC. of
595 Madison Avenue, New York, NY 10022.

Copyright © 1995 by Leo Kessler

All rights reserved.
The moral rights of the author to be identified as author of
this work have been asserted by him in accordance with the
Copyright Designs and Patents Act 1988.

British Library Cataloguing in Publication Data

Kessler, Leo
   Breakout from Stalingrad
   I. Title
   823.914 [F]

ISBN 0-7278-4804-6

Typeset by Palimpsest Book Production Limited,
Polmont, Stirlingshire
Printed and bound in Great Britain by
Hartnolls Ltd, Bodmin, Cornwall.

"Blow the bugle, beat the drum!
Clear the street, here comes the Wo-tan!
Steel is our weapon,
Go hew through bone,
Blood our purpose,
Wotan hold close.
For Death is our Destiny."

The Marching Song of SS Assault Regiment WOTAN.

Author's Note

"*The frigging epic of Stalingrad!*" ex-sergeant Schulze used to snort whenever the subject of that great battle was brought up by his beer-swilling cronies after the war. "Great Crap on the Christmas tree, Stalingrad was just one big crock o' shit!"

He'd take a great gulp of his 'suds, usually half a litre at one go, and launch into his familiar tirade. "First yer got his nibs, that shit Adolf sending his Sixth Army all the way to Stalingrad. Just for prestige, that's all. He wanted to capture the city which carried the name of that Popov arsehole, Stalin. Then that la-di-da, von Paulus, manages to get his poor sods of stubble-hoppers surrounded. Some bloody general – him!"

The nasty taste of that hated name would be washed away with another swallow of beer, before Schulze could go on. "What did Adolf do? Did he allow the Sixth to withdraw while there was still shitting time? Not on yer frigging life! He ordered the poor, half-starved stubble-hoppers to fight on to the last man and the last frigging bullet. Well, in the end, they didn't have the bullets to fight with. 'Cos Fat Hermann" – he meant the enormously fat head of the *Luft*waffe, Hermann Goering – "couldn't keep his promise to keep the Sixth supplied by air. Probably too doped up – he spent half the day sniffing coke up his fat hooter with a jewelled tube. Once his lot even dropped a whole case of contraceptives. What did he think the stubble-hoppers of the Sixth was supposed to do – *fuck the Popovs to death!*"

Here Schulze was always wont to laugh, drain the last of his beer and follow it down with a shot of fiery *Korn* before continuing his litany of disgust. "Our boss, that knock-kneed, ex-chicken farmer Himmler was no better, making us of Wotan fight it out in the ruins while he was dicking his fat secretary in Berlin!" Schulze's broad honest face would contort with disgust and he would sneer, "Ner, the whole shitting lot of 'em was cracked from top to bottom. Our leaders – I've shat them! We had better lance-jacks in Wotan than that lot. And the result? Four hundred thousand of the poor shits taken prisoner by the Popovs that year, were looking at the taties from below before the war was out."

"But you came out of Stalingrad in one piece, Schulzi," someone would always object, hurriedly ordering a fresh round of 'suds' at the same time.

"Yer," Schulze would reply slowly, mind obviously on other times. That old light would flash in his blue eyes, faded now most of the time or red with drink, "*but we was Wotan, wasn't we? . . .*"

Schulze is dead now these several years, dying the way he had always wanted to go, pleasuring an eighteen-year-old whore when he was in his mid-seventies. But we have enough of his story and those priceless *Obersturmbannfuhrer* von Dodenburg Papers, now kept at the German Army's own university at Hamburg, to piece together the real history of what happened at that Russian city in 1942. As Schulze always maintained, it was no 'epic'. Rather it was one of moral cowardice, treachery and counter-treachery. Not a pleasant story at all. But in that year, half a century ago now, there were no pleasant stories . . .

L.K. Bleialf, Germany, 1994.

PART ONE

The Trap

"We're caught in a pisspot and now they're gonna piss on us from a great height."

    Sgt Schulze to Cpl Matz, November 1942

Chapter One

Field Marshal von Paulus trembled. His face was unshaven and drawn. In the last three months he seemed to have aged ten years. Now, as he stood in the middle of the freezing cellar to address his officers, the Russian guns outside – all five thousand of them – thundered yet once more. The whole building shook and trembled like a live thing under that tremendous impact.

Von Paulus, commander of the German Sixth Army, did not seem to notice. He raised the paper he held in his gloved hand, which trembled slightly, and said, "On twenty-third November 1942, I sent this message to the Fuhrer, gentlemen." He cleared his throat: "*Mein Fuhrer*. Since receipt of your wireless signal of 22 November, the situation has developed with extreme rapidity. Ammunition and fuel are running short. I must forthwith withdraw all the divisions from Stalingrad itself and considerable forces from the nothern perimeter of the Pocket. In view of this extreme situation, I request you to grant me complete freedom of action."

Slowly, very slowly, von Paulus raised his head like a man who was infinitely weary. He stared at his officers, whose breath fogged the air in the freezing cold. They looked back at him in tense expectation. All of them knew they couldn't hold out much longer in the Pocket: a quarter of a million German and Allied soldiers trapped in a vast plain of snow and the ruins of Stalingrad. Had the Fuhrer approved the plan to break out while there was still time?

Von Paulus let them wait. Outside, the Russian guns had been joined by the 'Stalin organs', great rocket guns that tore the morning air apart with the hideous, banshee-like shrieks of their projectiles.

Finally the Field Marshal spoke after what seemed an age. "His answer came back at zero eight hundred hours this morning." With difficulty von Paulus switched the papers he held in his gloved hands. "Commander German 6th Army, Stalingrad," he read in a cracked, hoarse voice, "You will hold out to the last man and the last bullet. Signed Hitler." Von Paulus' voice broke. For a moment he looked as if he might let the papers drop from his shaking hand. But he caught himself in time. "So that is the situation, *meine Herren*." He continued in a quavering voice, "We must hold the Pocket till there are further orders."

Handsome, aristocratic General von Seydlitz-Kurzbach, commander of the 94th Infantry Division, who had what looked like a woman's scarf wrapped around his head to keep out the cold, wiped the dewdrop off the end of his blue nose, and snorted. "But this is madness, Field Marshal! We are trapped in a Pocket eighty kilometres broad, with the nearest German troops some two hundred kilometres away. Our allies, holding the southern front of the Pocket, those trashy Rumanians, Hungarians and the Italian spaghetti-scoffers, will pick up their heels and run for their lives once the Ivans attack in strength. Then the Sixth Army will be finished – *kaputt*!"

There was a murmur of agreement from the other officers present. From outside came the rattle of musketry.

The Russians were attacking yet once again under the cover of that tremendous barrage.

Seydlitz-Kurzbach looked almost pleadingly at the Army Commander. "Disobey the order, sir," he urged. "Break out now, while there's still time."

"Here, here," the others chanted eagerly, as the cellar walls shuddered and trembled under the impact of a salvo of rockets slamming into the iron-hard earth close by.

"Some of us would certainly make it back to von Manstein's' army back there. We've still got armour," Seydlitz-Kurzbach indicated Colonel Geier at the back of the cellar stroking his enormous nose which gave him the nickname of 'Vulture' among his SS troopers. "Geier's SS Assault Regiment Wotan could take the point. They'd get us through, I'm sure. If –" Abruptly the aristocratic General stopped short. He could see that von Paulus wasn't really listening.

The field marshal shook his head slowly like a very old man might. "We cannot disobey the orders of our beloved Fuhrer," he said with an air of finality. "Now you must return to your command. Our information is that the Russians will launch a full-scale attack just before last light – say – fifteen hundred hours. We must be ready."

Seydlitz-Kurzbach opened his mouth as if to protest, then thought better of it. Instead he clicked to attention like the rest of the officers.

Casually von Paulus touched his gloved hand to his battered cap. They were dismissed.

Subdued and worried, the officers filed out, clattering up the stone stairs out of the cellar and into the ruined, shell-shattered house above. It was snowing again, big wet flakes falling from a grey sky, as if they would keep in falling for ever. Still the supply planes were trying to get down and deliver their precious cargoes. For without the supplies brought by the 'Auntie Jus' – as the three-engined transport planes were nicknamed – the trapped men wouldn't last another twenty-four hours.

The Vulture buried his head deeper in his fur collar and fixed his monocle more firmly in his right eye. The fool of a pilot shouldn't circle much longer, he told himself, or the Ivans would have him. The Ivan Yak fighters and anti-aircraft artillery were always on the lookout for the supply planes. They knew that if they couldn't break into the Pocket, they'd starve the garrison into surrender in the end. Already von Paulus's army was down to one third of the normal rations. Daily they consumed ever more of their mules and horses. Now the loaves that the quartermaster's sections managed to produce contained more sawdust from sawn-up railway sleepers than they did flour.

His second-in-command, Major von Dodenburg, cap tilted at its usual rakish angle, appeared out of the whirling wall of white. He saluted and said almost immediately, harshly handsome face set and worried, "What's the drill, sir?"

The Vulture didn't bother to return the salute. It took too much effort and he was trying to conserve his strength. "There is no drill," he rasped in that harsh Prussian voice of his, "at least at the top. The Fuhrer has ordered us to fight to the last man and last bullet." His huge beak of nose wrinkled with contempt. "Like something out of a five groschen novelette, and Paulus, his creature, tamely accepts the edict." He stopped short and peered through the whirling snow.

The pilot of the 'Auntie Ju' had decided to make a go of it. Now the old-fashioned Junkers transport was racing across the snow, throwing up a great white wake, throttling back mightily. Already the pathetic crowds of wounded, surrounded by the 'chaindogs' armed with machine pistols, were shuffling forward, frantic to get aboard the plane, which would take them out of the hell of Stalingrad. In vain the military police, chaindogs, as they were known, from the metal plates of office they wore round their necks, blew their whistles angrily and fired off warning bursts into the air. The wounded didn't notice. Their gaze was fixed hypnotically on the plane.

"Poor wretches," von Dodenburg said feelingly, as he watched a soldier whose two legs had been blown off and who was now propelling himself forward on a little home-made cart, leaving a trail of blood behind him in the snow as he went.

"Another seven days here under these conditions and Wotan won't be much better," the Vulture observed grimly. With disgust he watched as an officer, obviously not wounded, offered the sergeant in charge of the chaindogs, a large wad of notes to let him get on to the plane now approaching.

With one last burst of noise, the plane skidded to a stop. Frantically the mob of wounded, some throwing away their crutches, fought and struggled to get through the cargo hatch, as the crew began dropping crates of supplion to the snow. The chaindogs stood back hastily. They knew the mob of panic-stricken wounded would trample them to death if they didn't.

Now the pilot who hadn't left the plane was beginning to rev his engines once more. *"They're taking off!"* the frantic mob shrieked. "They're taking off without us. They struggled forward once more. The man with no legs fell from his homemade trolley. He disappeared beneath the feet of the frantic mob.

"The Greater German Army, in the winter of 1942,

7

Russia," the Vulture observed cynically, polishing his monocle which had steamed up already in the biting cold.

"Poor swine," von Dodenburg said pityingly, as the plane began to roll forward once more, with wounded men clinging on to the tail and fuselage desperately. "They know it's their last chance—"

He stopped short. Like a hawk from hell, a stubby Yak had appeared from the snowstorm. Now it barrelled towards the heavily laden transport at four hundred kilometres an hour. Its four machine guns set in the wings started to spit purple fire. Slugs ripped the length of the 'Auntie Ju's' fuselage. Wounded men fell screaming to snow, wounded yet again. Desperately the harassed pilot tried to take evasive action. To no avail! Suddenly, startlingly, just as the plane had become airborne, the starboard engine burst into angry flame. For a moment the pilot fought to maintain control. He didn't succeed. The nose tipped. Next instant the Junkers hit the ground. It exploded at once. Flame seared the length of the fuselage like a great angry blowtorch. Men fell writhing and twisting into the snow, trying – in vain – to put out the all-consuming flames.

Von Dodenburg moved as if he were going to run for the burning plane. The Vulture caught him just in time. *"Too late!"* he roared as with one last great *crump* that seemed to go on for ever, the petrol tanks went up and the plane disintegrated in a glittering burst of molten metal.

Von Dodenburg groaned. But the Vulture was unmoved by the sight, the dead and the dying, the bodies, charred and shrinking rapidly in that tremendous blue heat, the absolute chaos, Instead he said slowly, as if thinking aloud, "This could be our last chance –

definitely." He dug his face deeper into the warmth of his fur collar. "All right, von Dodenburg, let's get back to Wotan. There is some planning to be done, my friend . . ."

Chapter Two

Cautiously, very cautiously, Sergeant Schulze of SS Assault Regiment Wotan raised a fist like a small steam shovel. In it he grasped a stick with a glove stuck on its point. Behind him in the long trench, one of the kitchen bulls was hacking at a sawdust loaf with an axe. Around him, a dozen Wotan troopers watched as if mesmerized, their eyes full of longing, as he hacked the frozen bread into slices. One slice and a tiny piece of mule flesh was to be their sole ration for this freezing November day.

"I'll shit in my boot before I eat a bit o' donkey's arse and half a sleeper," Schulze had snorted in disgust when the kitchen bull had crawled up to the frontline to announce this was going to be the day's rations. "Mrs Schulze's handsome son needs more than that – less than a bit of Yid foreskin docked by the chief rabbi – to line his precious innards!"

To which his long-time running mate, wizened, one-legged Corporal Matz had said, "You're lucky, old house. They say that the Macaronis," he meant Germany's Italian allies, "are scoffing their own stiffs."

Sergeant Schulze had shrugged his huge shoulders carelessly. "What can yer expect from a lot of frigging foreigners. They don't know no better. Just like the frigging French. They eat frogs out of a pond and make love with their frigging tongues." He had spat drily into the hard frozen snow. "Let's get on with it."

Now, while Corporal Matz prepared to flash a quick look through his binoculars from the far end of the trench, Schulze raised his stick. The dirty white glove broke over the parapet. Schulze licked his chapped lips in anticipation.

Crack! The glove tumbled to the bottom of the trench. Schulze felt the reverberations of the sniper's bullet rush tingling down his brawny arm.

Matz shouted excitedly. "Got the shitehawk!" He lowered his glasses.

"Frigging well nailed him first time!"

Schulze pushed his way through the hungry troopers staring fascinated at the kitchen bull with the axe. "Where?" demanded.

"Brick shithouse at three o'clock," Matz answered. "The front wall's gone. But they've put a bit o' tin in its place. He's under that. He's using smokeless powder. But I spotted the movement all right."

"You'll have a movement – *out of yer ass*, if you've got it wrong," Schulze snarted threateningly, but he knew Matz had the keenest eyesight of any man in the Regiment. He wouldn't get it wrong. "All right." He stroked his unshaven chin with fingers that looked like hairy pork sausages. "Now we've got to smoke the Popov and his pea-shooter out without getting ourselves knocked off."

Matz looked worried suddenly. "Perhaps we'd better call it off, Schulzi," he said. "You know them Ivan snipers. They're cunning arses-with-ears."

Schulze thrust a big thumb at his own massive chest. "Well, ape-turd, we've just got to be more cunning, ain't we? "He patted the little man's helmet like a fond mother

11

might do the head of a silly child. "You know them Popov snipers. They get the best fodder of any troops in the Popov army." He licked his lips in anticipation. "They have to stay out for twenty-four hours, so they get plenty of real grub with 'em." He tapped the side of his brick-red, dripping nose, "Besides, my little asparagus Tarzan, they also have the – *you know what*." He spelled out the words slowly, as if they were of the greatest importance.

Now it was Matz's turn to lick his lips in anticipation. "You mean firewater, Schulzi?"

"I do indeed, my little bird-brained friend. All them Popovs tank up with vodka before an attack. I reckon them snipers get the best firewater of the lot. Now the question is – how are we going to get our greedy little flippers on the fodder and firewater, eh?" He beamed at his running-mate.

Behind them the kitchen bull had finished cutting up the frozen rations. Someone was groaning, "But I've lost my gnashers. I can't eat that stuff with my gums."

"Tough titty," the kitchen bull sneered. "Self-inflicted wound, losing yer biters. I should turn yer in to Creeping Jesus." He meant Wotan's adjutant, who wore rubber soles on his boots so that he could creep up on some unsuspecting trooper doing something he shouldn't do. Morosely the toothless trooper started to suck the frozen bread.

Schulze answered his own question. "We need a decoy, that's what we need. *You!*"

"*Me*? Why frigging me?"

"Cos, Matzi, you're a lowly corporal and I'm a frigging high-level sergeant. Nuff said?"

"Nuff said," Matzi agreed somewhat morosely. "All right, let's frigging well go on with it."

Schulze slapped him heartily on the shoulder and nearly knocked him clean out of the trench. "That's the way to talk. Like men who've got a bit of spirit. Come on. *Los*. Can't wait to get my choppers on all that lovely Popov fodder."

Hesitantly, very hesitantly, Corporal Matz started to raise his helmeted head above the parapet, while Sergeant Schulze grinned encouragingly from the other end of the trench, rifle butt tucked into his shoulder. "Don't flash yer frigging biters at me," Matz said grimly, "concentrate on the frigging Ivan sniper. Here we go." He popped his head above the parapet.

Crack! Matz reeled back, face struck by bits of frozen earth and snow. The sniper's bullet had missed by millimetres.

But Schulze's didn't. It bored through the tin protecting the sniper's hide and struck home in solid flesh. There was a high-pitched shriek and the sniper's rifle tumbled to the ground from suddenly lifeless fingers.

"*Got the shit!*" Schulze roared. "Come on." He sprang from his hiding place and, holding his rifle in his mighty paw like a child's toy, he doubled across the snowfield. With one great kick, he booted the tin to one side and fell on the still form curled up on the ground, already patting the dead sniper's thick wadded jacket for loot. Abruptly he stopped, as if his fingers had been burned.

"What's up?" Matz gasped.

"*He's got tits*," Schulze exclaimed in wonder. "The sniper's got female tits."

"Great crap on the Christmas tree!" Matz said and stared down in open-mouthed amazement at the ample bosom swelling from underneath the thick Red Army shirt. "You're frigging well right, Schulzi – he has got plenty of wood before the door."

"*She*," Schulze corrected him routinely, beginning to recover from his shock.

"What a waste," Matz said, as Schulze now began to loot the body in search of 'fodder' and 'fire-water', "women are meant to dance the mattress polka with men, not shoot the poor sods. And look at that rifle," he indicated the dozen or so notches carved in the dead sniper's rifle butt. "She put plenty of poor old hairy-assed stubble-hoppers under the frigging sod."

Schulze nodded and, uncorking the bottle of vodka he had just found in the dead woman's back pocket took a hefty slug of it while Matz watched in greedy anticipation . . .

Watching them and the rest of the frozen undernourished Wotan troopers, von Dodenburg, making his usual early morning inspection of the Regiment's frontline positions, told himself something had to give soon. The long-suffering troopers couldn't stand much more of this. Thoughtfully he started to trudge back over the frozen creaking snow, while behind him the enemy guns started to thunder once more, heralding another day of hunger, misery and sudden death.

Wotan had been trapped in the Pocket for nearly a month now. Unlike the infantry, the frontline infantry, they had not suffered very severe casualties because von Paulus had declined to use the Regiment's armoured vehicles in battle. Besides, the Sixth Army had not sufficient fuel to carry out extensive tank operations. Still, the men suffered and died from other causes.

Sentries had been found frozen solid, killed by the murderous night cold. Mechanics who were careless enough to touch metal with their bare hands, found their flesh ripped away by the contact. Men had been discovered trapped and moaning in the makeshift latrines, their testicles frozen to the metal seats. As Schulze had quipped with a melodramatic shudder, "I'm willing to sacrifice everything for the Fuhrer, but not my balls!" Already Creeping Jesus, the hated adjutant, had asked for the death penalty to be imposed on two soldiers who had shot off their toes in an attempt to be sent back to the rear while there was still time.

"No," von Dodenburg told himself as he clambered into the volkswagen jeep, the driver gunning the engine to prevent it stalling in that biting cold, Wotan was still an effective fighting force. But how long would it remain effective under these terrible conditions. "All right, driver," he said aloud. "Let's get over to regimental HQ. The CO's holding an officer's conference at zero nine hundred." He forced a weary grin to the young driver, who like the rest was muffled up to the eyes in bits and pieces of both military and looted civilian clothing. "And you know what the Chief is like with anyone who's late?"

The driver returned the Major's grin, or at least von Dodenburg thought he did because he couldn't see much of the former's face. "Yessir. I know. I've heard him say, more than once, he'd have the eggs off'n anyone who's a second late for one of his conferences – *with a blunt razor blade!*" The young driver emphasized the words.

Von Dodenburg laughed hollowly. "Not a very pleasant thought to start off the day. All right. *Los!*"

The jeep began to bump over the snowfield, skirting the hillocks which housed the mass graves of those killed in the previous October when all Germany had rung to the news that the Sixth Army had virtually captured all of that great Volga city which bore the name of the hated Soviet dictator – Stalingrad. Now, von Dodenburg thought grimly, as they neared the former tractor factory which housed the armoured vehicles and regimental HQ of Wotan, that great victory had been turned into a terrible defeat. Would this be the end of Wotan? As the driver braked to a halt, that was one overwhelming question that the handsome young officer, with his rakishly tilted cap didn't dare attempt to answer.

Chapter Three

"*Stillgestanden!*" Creeping Jesus ordered, his breath fogging in the freezing air within the great factory hall.

The score of so of Wotan officers, many of them wrapped in civilian fur coats and pieces of captured Russian uniforms, which were better than the German, creaked wearily to attention.

Creeping Jesus, tall and weedy, his shifty dark eyes everywhere, turned and saluted the Vulture, who as usual was stroking his monstrous beak of a nose thoughtfully. "*Die Offiziere melden sich zur Stelle, Obersturmbannführer,*" he reported precisely, as if he were back at Wotan's depot in Berlin and not in this freezing waste of a battlefield.

Casually the Vulture returned his salute and ordered the officers to stand at ease. Behind the line of officers, a lone corporal in dark overalls and wearing huge felt boots over his own, was shuffling from vehicle to vehicle to light the tar pots beneath their engines. It was the only way to prevent their motors from seizing up permanently.

"*Meine Herren,*" the Vulture rasped, peering from face to face through the monocle he affected, though his sight was perfect, "I was at the C-in-C's briefing this morning." He let the words sink in, as the young officers stared at him, a faint hope beginning to glow in their strained faces.

The Vulture knew why. They expected him to announce that they were going to break out. He could understand them perfectly well. What would he give to be in Berlin right now, dressed in mufti, clean, warm and perfumed, searching the street outside the Hotel Adlon for those beautiful boys with their tight trousers and plucked eyebrows who were his private delight and only vice. Besides there was no promotion to be gained in Stalingrad. The Fuhrer never rewarded defeat and Stalingrad was going to be a defeat. Of that he was sure.

"In his infinite wisdom," he continued, "the Fuhrer has ordered we must stay here to the last bullet and the last man."

The announcement shocked the officers. Fervent, even fanatical, National Socialists as they all were, they could not refrain from showing their disappointment. Someone moaned. Another officer said in shaky voice, "But that is impossible!"

"It is impossible, I agree," the Vulture said and added with a look of cynical pleasure on his face at their disappointment. "But then the word of the Fuhrer is law."

Under a Tiger tank, the corporal lighting the tarpots intoned mournfully, as if to himself, "'Crap,' said the King and a thousand assholes bent and took the strain – for in them days, the words of the King were law."

With difficulty, von Dodenburg restrained himself from smiling. The mechanic had hit the nail on the head. Instead, he shot the man a black look. The latter wiped the dewdrop from the end of his nose and got on once more with his tarpots.

"However, gentlemen," the Vulture continued, the cynical look still on his cruel, perverted face, "we of

Wotan have always been somewhat of a law to ourselves, havent we?"

"Hear, hear," Creeping Jesus responded with fake heartiness.

Von Dodenburg frowned. He knew what the Vulture was up to and he didn't like it. But for the time being he said nothing.

"So gentlemen," the Vulture said, "I'm telling you, and you must tell your men, that Wotan must be prepared to take desperate measures when the time comes. And you can rest assured that time will come – and come soon. To merely exist, the Sixth Army needs five hundred tons of supplies each day. Do you know what has come in so far this day?" The Vulture answered his own question. "Exactly fifty tons, including three whole crates of Parisians." He meant contraceptives.

The officers laughed and the Vulture rasped, "What does the High Command expect us to do – *fuck the Popovs to death?*"

The officers laughed again. But von Dodenburg remained unmoved. He knew the Vulture of old. He was getting the officers into the right mood for his own purposes.

"Need I say more?" the Vulture continued. "The Stalingrad garrison won't last another week on that rate of re-supply. There are already cases of cannibalism among those glorious and brave allies of ours, the Italians, and our people's morale is badly shaken. There have been generals, yes generals who have been found trying to bribe their way onto the planes taking back the wounded to von Manstein's command!"

The officers gasped.

"Yes, it's true. Things are falling apart rapidly." He pointed a long forefinger at them, well manicured and as always painted with gleaming lacquer – even in the

The situation in Stalingrad, November 1942

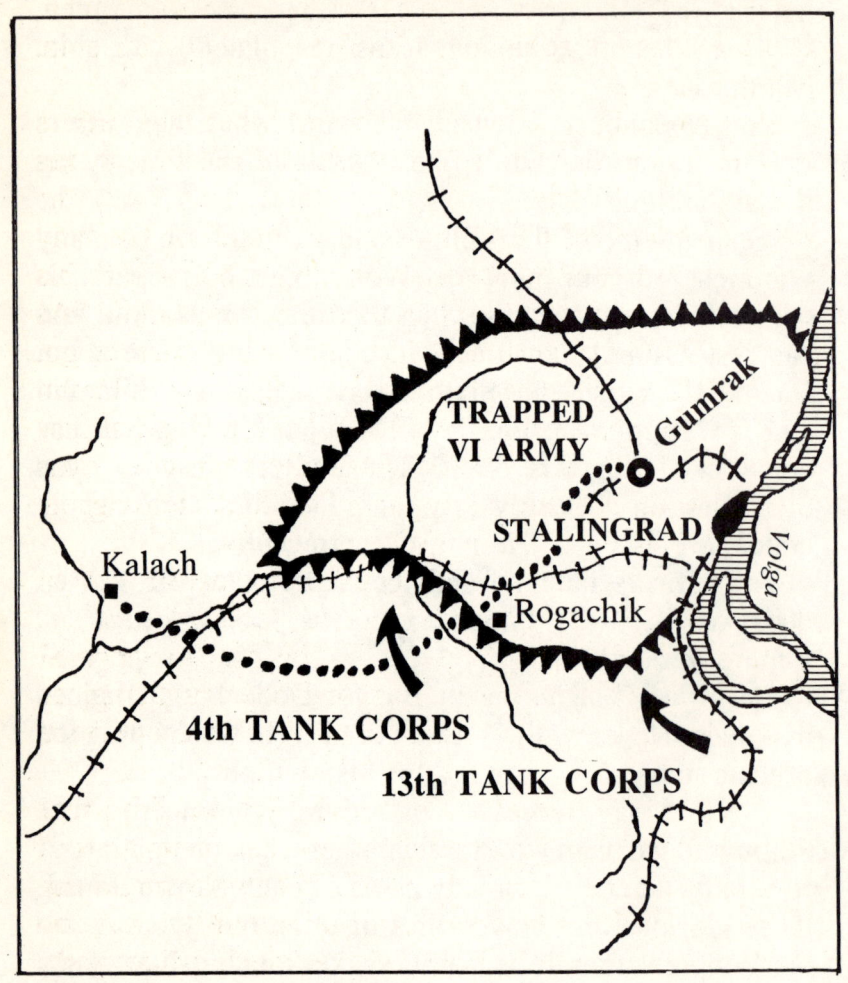

The Situation in Stalingrad, November 1942

hell of Stalingrad, the Vulture was not prepared to allow his standards to lapse. "But I can assure you, gentlemen, that Wotan is not going to go down with the sinking ship. No sir!"

Wan smiles spread over the faces of his young hearers at that supremely confident statement. None of his listeners particularly liked the Vulture. They knew he was perverted and had no interest in Wotan or the holy creed of National Socialism. His only interest was his own self-advancement. As he had often declared, "As soon as I get my general's stars, just as my father got his, I shall settle down to a nice easy office job in Berlin as a rear echelon stallion – and not have a single worry to put a wrinkle on my noble brow." But they knew, too, that when the Vulture set his mind to do something, he usually managed to bring it off.

"Now then," the Vulture continued, "we've got to make plans – contingency plans."

At his side, Creeping Jesus nodded his head in approval and rubbed his hands, which he was always doing, as if they were dirty and needed washing, which perhaps they did.

Von Dodenburg nodded his head, "Oh yes," he told himself, "Creeping Jesus would be all for doing a rapid bunk when the time came." He was a notorious coward. He always did his best never to go anywhere near the frontline if he could help it. "Far too much office work, dear fellow," he would usually twitter. "Love to be up there with the men – eating my heart out to get away from all this damned paperwork. But someone's got to do it, I suppose."

"As all of you know," the Vulture lectured them, "The point of von Manstein's German positions is at the village of Kalach, some twenty kilometres from the Russian line surrounding us." He clapped his hand and Creeping Jesus hurried away to return with a map which he propped up against the turret of the nearest Tiger tank.

The Vulture poked at it with the bayonet he carried these days. He reasoned that if he wore a bayonet, any Russian sniper wouldn't pick him out as a German officer; they always inclined to shoot officers first, then the lower ranks. "Here, we are just outside Gumrak Air Field, through which, as you know, all the supplies come. Here there is plenty of food, ammunition, and more importantly, fuel. All of it securely locked away for a rainy day by those fat gentlemen of the Quartermasters' Corps." He looked at their young faces knowingly.

Von Dodenburg knew what that look meant. In a time of crisis, the Vulture would take whatever he wanted, by force, if necessary. The quartermasters were universally hated for their greed and their determination not to part with any stores, if they could help it, as if the supplies belonged to them personally.

"Now," the Vulture went on, "we're virtually in the centre of the Pocket and fairly safe for the time being. It is my guess that when the Ivans attack, they will do do so on our southern flank – here – held by that rabble of Hungarian gypsies, Rumanian fiddlers and Italian spaghetti-scoffers. The Popovs know that that bunch will break first. So in any withdrawal, we must keep the River Karpovka – here – to our left. It will afford us some protection from a surprise attack by the enemy."

Von Dodenburg's frown deepened. The Vulture was spelling out exactly what *he* was going to do, whether von Paulus liked it or not. He was going to disobey the Fuhrer's order and pull back when the time came.

"Our breakout position," the Vulture went on, "will be – here," he pointed again with the tip of the bayonet, "just north-west of Marinovka. Till then I shall attempt to keep Wotan clear of any fighting. We shall need all our strength for the breakthrough and the withdrawal to von Manstein's positions at Kalach." Suddenly he looked grim. He stroked that monstrous nose of his as if he had just become aware of the magnitude of the task ahead. But he pulled himself together rapidly, saying, "From now onwards, gentlemen – comrades, we shall be on a permanent sixty minutes' alert. All vehicle motors will be turned over three times a day so that they start instantly in an emergency. I know that uses up fuel, but let that be my worry. All troops will be expected to mount up and move out in that hour. Anyone whose vehicle won't start will be left behind. Is that clear?"

That made the young officers sit up. Von Dodenburg knew why. Even when the engines did start, sometimes the vehicles wouldn't move because they were frozen solid to the ground.

"Each tank commander will take a full complement of panzer grenadiers with him on the deck of the tank. So that they don't freeze to death, the tank commanders – you – must ensure that they have all available warm clothing. In short," the Vulture concluded, "from this moment on, we must be prepared to move out at an hour's notice. There's no more time. Then it will be, as the Wotan's fighting motto has it, *march or croak!*" He flashed a look around their young worried faces. "Questions?"

Von Dodenburg raised his hand quietly.

"Yes, von Dodenburg?"

"Sir, do you intent to break out *without* orders from Field Marshal Paulus?"

Creeping Jesus shot von Dodenburg an angry glance, but the latter ignored him and continued. If you do so, sir," he persisted, "won't that be generally regarded as high treason?"

The Vulture stared at von Dodenburg as if he were seeing him for the first time. Then he said very slowly, as if his mind were on other things, "I think I shouldn't answer that question at the moment, von Dodenburg. But I'll let you know in due course."

Creeping Jesus waited no longer. Face excited at the thought that Wotan would soon be breaking out, he cried, "Commanding Officer on parade, attention – *salute*!"

Then they were gone, leaving von Dodenburg alone with the corporal mechanic, staring at the spot where the Vulture had stood, telling himself that for the first time in its history, Wotan was going to run away . . .

Chapter Four

An icy wind swept across the infinite white waste of snow. It slashed the watchers' red-gleaming faces with razor-sharp particles of ice. Time and time again, they blinked their eyes to force away the tears. Soon they knew the quartermaster bulls would be going across to the log hut on their way for their breakfast. Already they could smell the delightful aroma of real bean coffee coming from the place. Now they couldn't afford to slacken their watch. It was crucial. Time was going to be of the essence soon.

A sickly yellow winter sun slid slowly over the horizon. It hung there weakly, as if undecided whether to stay. Long black shadows ran across the steppe. Over the Russian lines a kilometre away, bright scarlet lights started to blink like the doors of giant furnaces suddenly being opened. A second later there was an angry rumble, followed an instant later by a great baleful roar. The dawn hate had commenced yet once again.

The two watchers ignored the barrage. They had become used to it by now. Instead they held their frozen, bearded faces to the sun, desperate to catch the slightest warmth, their breath fogging the icy air.

The gates of the quartermaster compound creaked open. Well-nourished quartermaster bulls in clean, thick uniforms, mounted on shaggy *panje* ponies which cantered crisply across the frozen snow, headed for their breakfasts in the log hut. Behind them streamed and stumbled the Russian prisoners who worked in the stores. Emaciated, eyes blazing from skeletal faces, dressed in rags, they fought to be first at the troughs into which the cooks were now pouring buckets of steaming swill, urged on by German guards wielding knouts.

"Poor Popov shits," Matz whispered. "They get even worse fodder than we do."

"Yer," Schulze snarled. "But those shitehawks on the gee-gees get enough grub. Look the nags are bending in the middle under the weight of those bulls."

Matz hawked and spat drily into the frozen snow. "What d'yer expect, Schulzi?" he said. "They're quartermaster bulls aren't they? Quartermaster and kitchen bulls never go hungry. They're born frigging mean. They wouldn't even give yer the crud from beneath their frigging fingernails."

Schulze nodded his agreement and then tensed as the last of the riders started to trot by their hiding place. "Half a litre of good fart soup," the bigger of the two was saying to his comrade, "a nice length of salami, and then a man's really ready for a bit o' the beaver. That's the fodder to put strength into a man. By God and all His Holy Triangles, I've got so much ink in my fountain pen, I don't know frigging know who to write to first!"

His comrade, also well-nourished, his face glowing with well-fed, rude health, laughed easily and said, "I thought you had enough Popov beaver the other night. They ain't pretty them Popov women, but they certainly do know how to perform the two-backed bear, old house."

His comrade nodded and they passed on.

Schulze waited till they were out of earshot before

exploding angrily, "Did you hear that, Matzi? Not only do they nick our fodder to fill their guts, but they've got gash as well! Christ on a crutch, I haven't had a diamond-cutter for weeks now. I just don't get enough fodder to get the old love-stick up."

Dourly Matz said, "Yer not the only one, yer know, Schulze. I can't even find my dick any more. It's shrunk right away. If this goes on, I'll have to piss out of my elbow soon."

But Schulze forgot his sexual problems. The quartermaster's depot would be deserted now for the next fifteen minutes while the guards and the prisoners fed. He knew that from the previous two mornings' observation of the place. At nine, the depot would be manned and the quartermasters would be dishing out rations to the various units calling for them. So they had exactly quarter of an hour to load up whatever they could lay their hands on into the quartermaster captain's own truck, which was kept running at this time of the day so that important personage could set off in a nice warm vehicle to inspect his various sub-units. As Schulze had told his weary, starving platoon just before he had left on the dawn raid, "This day, you bunch o'cardboard soldiers are gonna get yer biters into some real fodder for a change. Let's see if we can change yer back into real hairy-assed stubble hoppers agen."

Hurriedly the two of them doubled across the snow to the depot's back gate. As they expected, it was locked and chained. Schulze didn't hesitate. He had come prepared. He slipped the wire-cutters around the chain, grunted, heaved with his maasive shoulders and the chain snapped in two, as if it were made of thin wire instead of solid steel. "Here we go, Uncle Otto," he exclaimed happily as the big gate swung open invitingly. "Come on Matzi.

Los. I'd like to see the look on that fat quartermaster captain's ugly kisser when he sees that somebody has looted his precious store of goodies."

Matz needed no urging. He was already beginning to drool at the thought of all the delicacies which would soon be theirs. "Christ, Schulze," he said, "the chinwater's already soaking my collar. Let's be at it!"

Hurriedly they ventured into the nearest storehouse on the other side of the inner compound. "It's like frigging Christmas," Schulze breathed in awe as he stared momentarily around the vast room. It was packed with smoked meats of all kinds, great Westphalian sausages, the pig gut gleaming richly with fat, cured Parma hams that would need two men to lift, sides of bacon, just ready for the carving – and everywhere tins and even more tins. "Holy strawsack," Matz exclaimed, "look at that salami and that tinned bread, *white* bread, and that lump of smoked pork, oozing with lard. Schulzi, catch me. I think I'm going to have an orgasm!"

"Keep it to a frigging low roar," Schulze hissed warningly. "And don't stand around like a spare dick in a convent. Hop to it!"

Gleefully Matz 'hopped to it'. Swiftly they doubled back and forth loading the little truck, engine running sweetly, with the kind of food they hadn't seen for months, already visualizing the great feast they would have this night. Each time, the two of them, grinning like schoolboys just let out of a boring lesson, would knock the head of one of the many bottles of 'good Munich suds', as a happy Schulze called the Bavarian beer, and take a great gulp before tossing the bottle away.

Suddenly their progress came to a dramatic halt. They

were just lugging a side of frozen beef to the piled-high truck, which must have weighed nearly two hundred pounds, when an angry official voice demanded, "What in three devils' name is going on here, eh? What are you men up to?"

They turned startled, still holding the side of beef. A great ox of a man in the uniform of a captain quartermaster stood there, legs straddled, an automatic pistol in his elegantly gloved hand. His uniform was smart and pressed, sporting no decorations save the War Service Cross, Third Class. But he looked a real soldier not like the ragged wretches standing startled in front of him. He radiated an aura of soldierly well-being like a man who had never been hungry in his whole life and never intended to be, either.

"Well," he demanded when the two culprits didn't speak. He jerked up the muzzle of the pistol threateningly. "Come on, spit it out. *Raus mit der Sprache!* Who are you—" He stopped short suddenly when he spotted the black and silver armband of the Wotan on Schulze's sleeve. "Thieving shitting SS men from the celebrated Wotan, eh!" he exclaimed. "Well, gentlemen of the SS," the fat quartermaster sneered. "The German Army, to which you belong, though perhaps you don't seem to realise that, has a penalty for looting. And just in case you don't know what it is, I'm going to tell you. It is death—"

Schulze hit him with the side of beef. The quartermaster captain went down onto his knees, gasping and cursing. Schulze didn't give him a chance to recover. With a mighty kick, he sent the quartermaster's pistol flying across the frozen snow. Next moment he rammed his big knee into the quartermaster's groin. He grunted thickly. Suddenly the quartermaster's false teeth were bulging stupidly from his open gasping mouth, as he grabbed for his injured testicles.

"Come on!" Schulze yelled.

"The beef— !"

"Frig the beef! They're sending out the cavalry." He shoved Matz behind the wheel and tumbled inside the cab himself in the same instant that the furious quartermaster bulls came cantering over the snow, yelling wildly and firing their pistols as they rode to stop the thieves.

Matz slammed home first gear. Then they were moving fast – very fast. The 'cavalry' saw the danger. They tugged at their animals' bits. The little ponies reared up and flailed their forelegs with fear, as Matz drove straight at them, scattering bottles and tins over the sides of the truck as he hit the frozen hummocks of snow at speed. At the trough, the Russians cheered and cheered crazily, as if they themselves would soon be enjoying the stolen delicacies. Then they were gone, rolling back to the Wotan's lines, followed by a ragged volley of wild rifle fire, directed by a sobbing, toothless captain quartermaster who kept repeating, "I'll string them up if it's the last thing I ever do. They'll dangle for this . . ."

A kilometre away, relaxed now, swigging great slugs of stolen *Kognak*, Sergeant Schulze raised one huge haunch and let rip one of his long and not unmusical farts, which were renowned through the SS NCO corps, to say, "Matzi, we've done it. We've got the goodies and fucked a captain quartermaster bull." He finished the bottle with one last satisfying gulp and threw the 'dead soldier' carelessly through the window. "How many stubble-hoppers can say that – fucked a captain quartermaster of the Greater German Army?"

"Famous last words," Matz remarked at the wheel.

Suddenly he felt somber and apprehensive. He remembered what the fat quartermaster had said was the penalty for looting – death. He shivered – and it wasn't with the cold.

Chapter Five

"Stand at ease!" Creeping Jesus ordered in that mean voice of his, dark rat-like eyes flashing from one end of the parade to the other, threateningly.

Obediently the troopers relaxed in the centre of the great factory hall, the stamp of their boots echoing hollowly through the place. Outside, the Russian guns continued to boom, as they had been doing for twenty-four hours now.

Creeping Jesus, the adjutant, allowed the troopers to wait. He regarded such enforced long waits as a good tactic. It confused and worried private soldiers, he thought, especially if they had a guilty conscience, as this bunch of worthless scoundrels had. He could see it from the very faces of the thieving rogues. They were glowing and seemed fuller, obviously from the fodder that these criminals had stolen from the quartermaster's depot.

He cleared his throat ominously, or so he thought he did, and began. "I've had my eyes on you bunch of unmitigated rogues for some time now. To the man, you are troublemakers. I've long known that. Now some of you have had the great temerity to strike a superior officer when he was only trying to protect the supplies under his command. What do you have to say to that, eh?"

Standing in the front, eyes fixed on some object known only to himself, Sergeant Schulze farted. It was not one of his usual quite pleasant farts. No, this was a hard, rasping kind of a fart that was meant to be provocative.

Creeping Jesus' sallow face flushed an angry red. "Who did that?" he demanded. "Come on – out with it. That was clearly intended as dumb insolence. Not only are you men thieves who strike a superior officer, you are also men who would insult one of your own officers. Now who did that?" He peered angrily at their wooden faces.

But the men didn't return his look. Instead they gazed, for the most part, at the high ceiling, as if bored with the whole business, which made Creeping Jesus even more angry. Furiously he fumbled in the turn-up of his sleeve for his notebook and pencil. "I will have that disgusting man's name, even if you have to stand here all day until you tell me it. Come on now – who broke wind in that disgusting manner?"

"Captain Hirsch," von Dodenburg cut in gently from where he stood leaning against the side of a 60-ton Tiger tank which he had just inspected. "I suggest you get on with the business at hand." He nodded in the direction of the barrage, "Because somehow I doubt if we will be here in twenty-four hours' time. I think the enemy will take care of that." He gave Creeping Jesus a winning smile.

Creeping Jesus opened his mouth, as if he might object, then thought better of it when he saw the look in von Dodenburg's hard, light-blue eyes. Von Dodenburg was an arrogant swine who thought he could do just as he pleased because he'd won every decoration for bravery in the book. He was far too familiar with the men as well. Mentally he noted he would put von Dodenburg's name on the top of his personal shit-list. One day he'd get even with the swine. Aloud, he said, "Yessir. I shall get on with it." Creeping Jesus turned his attention to the men once more. "Now then," he snapped," I shall now have Captain Quartermaster Erle brought in. He is not feeling very well and will need some assistance. He will look at each man in turn and you will look directly at him. Is that understood. Once he identifies the culprit, that man will be arrested at once. Is that clear?"

There was a reluctant murmur of understanding from the ranks and von Dodenburg told himself he could guess already who the culprit would be. It would be either Matz or Schulze. They were the two most notorious scroungers in the whole of Wotan. But they were also two of his most experienced and reliable NCOs. They were men he could ill afford to lose. He couldn't let the chaindogs get their paws on Matz and Schulze. He tugged the end of his nose and wondered how he was going to save them when the captain quartermaster identified them, which he surely would.

The captain quartermaster was not that masterful figure he had been when it had been his ill-luck to encounter Matz and Schulze two days before. He was bent and carrying a stick, plus being supported by two burly chaindogs. He had a black eye and the right side of his face, where Schulze had heaved the side of beef at him, was green and swollen. As he shuffled forward with the aid of the military policemen, he kept one hand tightly clutched to his testicles, whether on account of pain or from fear that they might be attacked and savaged once more, the watchers didn't know.

"Holy strawsack," Matz chirped from the side of his mouth, "you don't frigging know yer own strength, Schulzi. Just look at his kisser."

"Just a playful tap," Schulze answered easily. "Don't know what they're making all the frigging fuss about."

The captain quartermaster coughed thickly and a trickle of blood appeared at the corner of his swollen mouth.

"He's consumptive as it is," Schulze said unfeelingly. "Probably infected all our fodder with his frigging germs."

"Hold yer frigging water," Matz hissed. "He's getting close."

Slowly, supported by the chaindogs, the injured officer made his way along the files, staring for what seemed a long time at each man before passing on. In the rear rank, Matz and Schulze did some quick thinking. They knew that as soon as the quartermaster bull identified them – and he surely would – Creeping Jesus wouldn't hesitate in having them arrested. As Schulze had cursed to Matz before the identification parade had started, "That shit-heel would turn in his own mother – if he ever had one – to the Gestapo. Then the clock'll really be in the pisspot." Matz had appeared to take the prospect carelessly: "So what? They send us back to Torgau Military Prison. Then, at least, we'll be out of this particular hell hole."

But that wasn't to be. In the very same instant that the injured captain quartermaster stopped in front of a wooden-faced Schulze, already trembling with rage as he recognized his assailant, the great door of the factory hangar was thrown open. The Vulture stood there, face red with excitement, eyes bulging out of his ugly head like those of a man demented, *"Alarm . . . alarm!"* he bellowed at the top of his voice. "Stand to everybody! The Ivans have broken through the shitting spaghetti-scoffers to the south . . . They're in full retreat. Stand to for action!"

"But sir," Creeping Jesus attempted to interrupt the Vulture, "We've just identified the criminal who struck poor Captain Erle here and looted his depot—"

"No time for that kind of nonsense now," the Vulture barked. "Wotan's going to need every manjack it can find."

Creeping Jesus balled his soft fists with suppressed rage and frustration but there was nothing he could do about it, as von Dodenburg strode across to the parade, winking knowingly at that big villian Schulze, to command, "All right, break ranks. At the double now. Secure your weapons and stand by for further orders." He turned and doubled urgently to where the Vulture was waiting for him.

"All right," Creeping Jesus snapped, "You heard the officer. Get on with it."

Schulze flashed Matz a look, "I think I just pissed in my boot," he said with a grin.

"What do yer mean – *think*?" Matz snapped returning the look. "I *know*, I did." Then like the rest they were away, running into the open, the helpless Captain Quartermaster and an enraged Creeping Jesus already forgotten as they realised instinctively that the last battle for Stalingrad had commenced.

It was a realisation that the Vulture had also already come to. Now as he stood there in the slowly drifting snowflakes, which muted the sound of the Soviet barrage a little, he snapped to von Dodenburg, "The next four hours or so will be critical. You understand that, von Dodenburg?"

Von Dodenburg, his mind racing electrically, nodded grimly. "If the C-in-C can't stabilize the Italian front with new troops – preferably German – by nightfall, the Ivans will pour more and more soldiers into the gap. They are much our superior at night fighting, and as far as I know the Italians never fight at night."

The Vulture forced a wintry smile. "Yes, the southern gentlemen will undoubtedly put all their energy into keeping on running this particular night." His smile vanished. "God knows where von Paulus will find fresh troops. The Sixth German Army is stretched to the limit as it is and the troops are decidedly unfresh."

"What is the latest from von Paulus' HQ, sir?" von Dodenburg asked, as red signal flares started to sail into the leaden sky to their front, indicating that the Russians were also attacking there. He guessed, however, this would be only a feint: an attempt to keep the German troops in their positions.

"Not much . . . The gentlemen of the purple stripe," he meant staff officers who wore the purple stripe of a staff-trained officer on their breeches, "inform us that the Ivans have carved a ten kilometre gap in the Italian front. They inform us, too, nothing will be done at this moment. There is no cause for alarm. The C-in-C has taken off in his personal plane to assess the Italian front." He laughed cynically. "As if a ten kilometre gap doesn't convince him that this is the final Soviet offensive. Nothing will be done until he returns and reports."

"So there isn't a general alert?" von Dodenburg asked quickly, realising that the Vulture had called the alert on his own responsiblity.

"Exactly. In time of battle, he who hesitates is lost. If Napoleon didn't say that, he should have done. Within twenty-four hours, my dear young friend, the Sixth German Army will start to disintegrate. Then it won't be just lowly colonels like myself who have to start making vital decisions, it will be corporals and private soldiers. Believe you me von Dodenburg, soon it's going to be every man for himself and the Devil take the hindmost. That is not going to happen to Wotan. Now let's get over to HQ and see if we can find out anything new about our flying C-in-C . . ."

Chapter Six

It seemed as if the whole Italian Army in Russia was on the move. Everywhere there were columns of horse-drawn transports blocking the few roads to the rear, moving with painful slowness. They were fleeing from the advancing Russians who were slaughtering, looting, pillaging and raping (there were many women with the Italians from their frontline brothels and the mistresses of the higher ranking officers). Hungry, frozen, exhausted and frightened, they plodded down the ice-glazed roads in the sub-zero temperatures. If they were lucky, they trundled westwards in farmcarts, covered with tarpaulins, through which chimneys had been poked for the stoves inside. It was a retreat of incredible suffering, akin to the retreat of Napoleon's *Grande Armee* from Moscow over a century before. But no one had any thought of easing his flight, even the elegant, perfumed staff officers when their cars broke down. The spectre of the ever-victorious Red Army and the horrific retribution they would wreak on those who had deigned to invade Holy Mother Russia, drove even the weakest ever onwards.

Once again, von Paulus' light plane came down low over the snowy waste to allow the field marshal to survey the fleeing Italians through his field glasses. This time the Italians were running, fleeing across the steppe, apparently at the sight of a single T-34 Russian tank. Hundreds of them, and most of them wore the feathered crest of the *Bersagliere*, one of Italy's elite regiments. Von Paulus shook his head and lowered his glasses, as if he could not bear to look any more. If the elite of Mussolini's army in Russia were running away, what could he expect from the rest? He touched his throat mike which connected him with the pilot and said wearily, "*Hauptmann*, take me back to HQ. I've seen enough."

For the rest of the flight back, von Paulus lapsed into a worried silence, as he pondered the same question time and time again. What was he going to do? But even when he landed and was motored straight away to his cellar headquarters, he had still not made that overwhelming decision, although he could see just how tense the situation was. Staff officers ran back and forth with undue haste for them. Telephones jingled constantly, and in the corner at a desk lit by a flickering candle, a worried staff major was staring at a map and barking into a phone at the same time, "But you must hold. It is imperative you do so. *HOLD!*"

But von Paulus, the veteran of two wars, noticed other signs of the panic soon to break out. Nearly every staff officer had a small case ready packed at the foot of his desk, and he didn't need a crystal ball to know why. The gentlemen of the Greater German General Staff were already packed ready to march into Soviet captivity. They might order the men to fight to the "last bullet and the last man", but *they* were certainly not going to do that.

"Sir,"

He turned startled.

It was Colonel Wilhelm Adam, his immensely tall adjutant. "What is it, Willi?" he asked.

"This. One of the operators has just taken it down. It's

from a speech just given in Berlin by Fat Hermann*." He sniffed contemptuously. "Absolute drivel, sir."

Von Paulus took the piece of paper and ran his eyes over it quickly. Goering had stated in his speech: "My soldiers. Thousands of years ago, in a tiny pass in Greece,stood a tremendously brave and bold man with three hundred soldiers: Leonidas and his three hundred Spartans . . . Then the last man fell . . . and now only the inscription stands: *'Wanderer, if you should come to Sparta, go tell the Spartans you found us lying here as the law bade us'* . . . Someday men will read, *'If you come to Germany, tell the Germans you saw us lying in Stalingrad as the law bade us.'*

Von Paulus looked up from the paper and Adam said, face filled with contempt, "They say that the fat fool had tears in his eyes when he said the words. He would have had real tears in his eyes if I had been there because I would have kicked him up his fat arse – hard."

Von Paulus nodded. "See that the men don't get to know about the speech. It's all too clear that he, perhaps even the Fuhrer, has written us off. What do they know of the conditions here at Stalingrad?" he asked bitterly. "Does the fat dope addict know that the cellars are full of wounded and dying, with hardly any medicine and only paper bandages to go over their wounds? That our rifles are freezing up? That we can't fire our cannon because we have no special winter grease to keep the lenses from freezing up? Does he damn well know that his own air force only delivered a hundred tons of supplies yesterday when we need five hundred—" He broke off, face red with anger.

With difficulty he contained himself as a staff officer

* Herman Goering, the immensely fat head of the German *Luftwaffe*.

rushed by, obviously in a panic, saying as he passed, "Three Italian divisions have been wiped out. Two more are not capable of any further resistance, Field Marshal."

Von Paulus shook his head like a man trying to wake up from a bad dream. "Nevertheless we must keep faith, Willi."

"Sir," the adjutant said woodenly.

"Have you got your pad there?"

The adjutant nodded.

"I want the following message to be sent to the Führer and distributed among the troops as well.

"Sir."

Von Paulus cleared his throat. Above, Stormovik dive-bombers were falling out of the sky, sirens shrieking shrilly, to launch their bombs on his HQ. But he dismissed the thought that the enemy now knew where his headquarters was and concentrated on the message to Hitler. "The Sixth Army," he commenced, "hails its Führer . . . The swastika flag is still flying above Stalingrad—"

Colonel Adam looked at his Chief, but von Paulus ignored the look and continued, "May our battle be an example . . . to the present and coming generations . . . that they must never capitulate . . . even in a hopeless situation . . . for then Germany will come out victorious . . . Hail my Führer . . . Paulus, Field Marshal . . ."

"Do you really want me to send this, sir? More importantly, do you want it distributed among the men?" Adam ventured. "They'll construe it in one way only. They'll realise that we – they – are lost, sir."

Von Paulus shrugged carelessly. "But *we* are lost, Willi. The Führer won't allow us to withdraw. So we must stay here and fight to the end."

Adam tried one more time. "But there can be no talk

of fignting to the end, sir. We'll run out of supplies and ammunition before that. The only end for the Sixth Army, sir, to put it brutally, will be surrender – shameful surrender."

"What is the alternative?"

Adam forced iron into his voice, angry at the Field Marshal's apparent apathy. "Disobey the Führer's order. Make the decision to withdraw whether Hitler likes it or not, sir. If you make that decision today, we still stand a fighting chance to reach von Manstein's lines." He clenched his fist, as if willing von Paulus to do as he suggested. "We shall suffer losses, great losses probably, but some of us will survive to fight another day."

"In ten generations of service to Prussia and Germany, a von Paulus has never disobeyed an order from above," von Paulus said doggedly. "My ancestors would turn in the grave if I did so."

Adam's long face flushed angrily. At that moment he could have shaken the field marshal out of his complacent apathy. "It is not a question of your personal honour, sir," he said icily. "It is a question of trying to save the lives of as many German soldiers as possible. Every man of your army has a wife, children, a mother. When they are lost, all those people back home will grieve for them. What is your personal honour against all that sorrow and misery?"

A flash of the old fire animated von Paulus' weary features, "You are forgetting your place, Adam," he snapped. "Remember you are talking to the C-in-C."

"I'm sorry, sir. But the time has come for plain speaking."

"Right, then you shall have it. I and my Sixth Army remains here till the end, whatever that end will be. There will be no withdrawal unless I am ordered to do so by the Führer. Now please ensure that message gets sent off."

"Yessir," Colonel Adam said and clicking to attention, he saluted.

Field Marshal von Paulus didn't seem to notice.

Shoulders bent as if in defeat, Colonel Adam left. The fate of the German Sixth Army had been sealed. When he had left, von Paulus buried his head in his hands and began to sob like a broken-hearted child . . .

Chapter Seven

"Well, there you are," the Vulture rasped contemptuously. He tossed von Paulus' message onto the mud floor of the HQ bunker. "Now we know where we stand. The Sixth German Army is about to sink up to its nose in the crap."

Creeping Jesus gave a nervous giggle at the remark. The Vulture shot him a hard look. He shut up immediately.

Outside, the guns were roaring in full fury. Even the blizzard raging, as if the snow would never stop, failed to drown the noise and fury of that tremendous barrage.

"The Macaronis are finished," the Vulture went on. "Now the Ivans are preparing to drive right into our left flank. In due course they'll do the same on our right flank. They'll link up and the Pocket will be split in two. It's clearly on the cards." He shrugged. "After that, the Ivans will split it into four. In fact, they won't stop until they have broken the Sixth into a worse collection of worthless soldiers and shattered positions than it is at this moment. Then what's left will surrender. And that fool von Paulus sends a message like this to the Führer. The man must be raving mad."

Von Dodenburg, listening gloomily to the Vulture's pessimistic analysis, knew he was right. The only strategy now was a fighting retreat back to link up with von

Manstein's army. Even in its present state, the Sixth Army was still a considerable force. It stood a fighting chance of making the link-up. Naturally the Führer never liked to give up ground which, as he put it, "had been purchased with German blood". Still, Von Dodenburg wiped the dewdrop off the end of his red, pinched nose and slung it angrily on the floor.

"Well, the time for decisions has come and I've already made them." He stared around at the other officers in the crowded HQ. "Each company will send out a raiding party immediately. They will break into stores and depots and take whatever the company commander deems is necessary for the breakout. Those two rogues, Schulze and Matz, are the kind of crooks you need for this type of operation. They've got a nose for loot." He looked directly at Creeping Jesus and the latter flushed and lowered his gaze. The Vulture grinned.

"Are you really going through with this?" von Dodenburg asked directly.

"*Naturlich*," the Vulture answered equally directly. "What do you think the Ivans will do to us when von Paulus surrenders, which he will? I'll tell you, von Dodenburg. We're Wotan and the elite of the SS." He drew a finger across his wrinkled, skinny throat. "*That*! The men will be dead within the hour. The Ivans'll probably take more time with the officers and it won't be very pleasant." He looked challengingly at von Dodenburg. "Well, what do you say to that? Are you prepared to sacrifice the Regiment, condemn it to a miserable death?"

Von Dodenburg knew the Vulture didn't give a damn about Wotan. He wanted to save his own neck so that he could obtain those precious major-general's stars. Hadn't he said often enough, "I don't care how many men I lose in battle, as long as they earn me my stars?"

"Aren't we running the risk of being charged with the act of desertion if we do as you suggest?" Von Dodenberg tried desperately, trying to find some way out of the impasse, knowing they couldn't abandon von Paulus' doomed army with a clear conscience.

"Perhaps," the Vulture conceded. "But in the débacle to come, who will worry about that? The main thing is that the Wotan, the SS's best armoured regiment, remains intact, ready to fight another day. That is what Berlin will concern itself with."

Von Dodemburg gave up.

The Vulture said, "Let's not waste any more time on the matter and idle chatter like a lot of old women." He looked at Creeping Jesus. "Get the raiding parties organized, Adjutant. Weather tells me that this snow storm is going to last a further three hours. I want to be out of here by then. The storm should give us cover till nightfall. That's all *meine Herren.*"

Now all was hectic activity. For the first time since Wotan had arrived at the Stalingrad front, the tanks and the half tracks were readied to leave the cover of the factory. Mechanics, sweating heavily despite the freezing cold and red-faced with the effort, cursed and swore as they cranked the huge handles to start the motors. Outside, the raiding parties ploughed through the knee-deep new snow searching for the supplies they needed for the breakout.

They fought their way through the Italians fleeing the shattered southern front. Frantic Italians of their crack infantry regiments who had already thrown away their weapons in their overwhelming, unreasoning fear. Mobile field brothels, the women drivers flogging their skinny-ribbed horses and old nags to keep them moving. One of the girls had given birth to a child. Now the dead, bloody baby lay wrapped in a newspaper at the side of the track. An Italian captain was running round in circles, howling at the leaden sky before slumping down exhausted in the snow and then commencing the crazed running once more. A dead general had shot himself in the mouth, the back of his head blown off. And paper, everywhere paper, was marking the trail of the fleeing columns.

Schulze shook his head more than once, as he led his raiding party forward, saying, "*Meschugge*, the whole frigging world is *meschugge* – *CRAZY*!"

'One Flipper', another of the raiding party, so named because he had lost his arm, grinned and said, the wet snow streaming down his brick-red face, "But we of Wotan ain't *meschugge*. We're gonna get out from under, Sarge."

Schulze nodded grimly. "Yer right there, One Flipper," he agreed. "We've survived a helluva lot o' shit in this war for Folk, Fatherland and Führer. We're gonna survive Stalingrad as well."

It was the same thought that animated the Vulture, as he strode purposefully around his command, barking out orders, snapping notes to Creeping Jesus who followed him everywhere, notepad in hand, complimenting men, threatening them, nodding his approval as the raiding parties came back with their booty – oil, petrol, food, ammunition, bread – all the things they would need if Wotan was going to reach von Manstein under its own steam.

"But what if von Paulus finds out we're abandoning the sinking ship?" von Dodenburg had objected. "Perhaps one of the raiding parties is apprehended and blabs?"

The Vulture had laughed scornfully. "What he could and would do would have to contend with this." With his gloved hand he had slapped the thick metal hide of the nearest Tiger tank. "Nothing – Russian or German – can stop a Tiger."

Von Dodenburg had stared at him aghast. "You mean, sir, you'd fire at your comrades?" he exploded.

The Vulture had nodded easily. "Why not? Now it's dog eat dog. If you want to see what German will do to German, stay behind and wait for the surrender, my dear friend." And with that he strode away, followed by a grinning Creeping Jesus.

By three o'clock that afternoon, with the snowstorm still raging furiously, Wotan was ready to march. Every vehicle was piled high with spares and stores. Panzer grenadiers huddled on the armoured monsters' decks, crouching behind heaps of clothing and bedding, knowing that it was going to be hellish cold. Still, they consoled themselves with the thought they were leaving the hell of Stalingrad. They were not going to leave their bones to bleach on this remote steppe so far away from the Homeland.

The great doors of the factory were thrown open. The snow howled inside in full fury. The Vulture, in the lead in his Volkswagen jeep, didn't seem to notice. He rolled his arm round three times, the signal for start up.

In the first Tiger behind him, von Dodenburg pumped his right arm up and down. "Roll 'em!" he yelled above the racket, coughing a little in the fumes streaming from the vehicles' engines.

Down below in the driver's compartment, Matz slammed home the first of the Tiger's many gears. There was a rusty squeak of tracks. Next to von Dodenburg, as the 60-ton monster started to move, Schulze yelled, "It's gonna be hairy, sir."

Von Dodenburg nodded but said nothing. He couldn't.

His mind was too full of the fact that SS Assault Regiment Wotan was abandoning the Sixth Army. Like thieves in the night, they were stealing away, the only armour that von Paulus possessed, leaving him and his men to their fate. He had a sour taste in his stomach. He didn't like it one bit.

The Tiger nosed its way out of the door. The great snowstorm engulfed it at once. One by one the other great metal beasts followed. Wotan had commenced its breakout.

"*What?*" von Paulus exploded, roused from his lethargy, "what did you say, Willi?"

Colonel Adam repeated the startling news.

"But this is impossible. 'In all the years of war, however hard the situation, the SS have always fought to the end. It's their motto, after all. 'Loyalty is my oath.'"

The big adjutant laughed hollowly. "In the case of *Obersturm-bannfuhrer* Geier, that doesn't seem to apply, sir. They've done a bunk – and that's that."

Von Paulus looked as if he might break down and cry at any moment.

Colonel Adam took pity on him. "Look, sir," he said urgently. "This disappearance of Geier's Wotan might be a blessing in disguise."

"How do you mean?"

"This. If the vaunted SS – the black guards – are retreating without orders, surely it is indicative of just how serious the situation is here at Stalingrad. Let the Führer know at once. There might still be a chance that he'll pull us back."

"Do you think so, Willi?" In his urgency von Paulus grasped the big adjutant's hand and pressed it hard.

"It's our last chance, sir."

"Then send this straight away to the Führer, Main HQ:

'SS Regt. Wotan deserted in the face of intense enemy pressure. Await orders. Von Paulus.'"

The C-in-C licked suddenly dry lips. "My God, Willi, we might be saved after all."

Adam looked up from his pad. "I'll pray that you're right, sir," he said earnestly, knowing that he had never prayed since he had left school at eighteen to join the army. But this dark November day, with the wind howling outside and the snow coming down in never-ending streams, he definitely would.

Chapter Eight

"*Himmelherrjeskarament!*" Hitler cursed in that thick Austrian accent of his, taking his hand away from the coat of his favourite dog, Blondi, as if the bitch's fur had suddenly become red-hot.

Colonel-General Jodl, his chief-of-staff, pale-faced and cunning-eyed, said appeasingly, "There might be some explanation for it – I am sure there is – but for the time being it appears that SS Assault Regiment Wotan has disappeared from the Stalingrad front." As was his wont, Jodl said the words without emotion or feeling, but his dark eyes were taking in Himmler, head of the SS, opposite him, who now, he thought, looked distinctly sick.

"How can such a thing be possible?" Hitler demanded, stuttering a little with rage. "The Wotan is the elite of the elite. I have decorated several of its officers personally. What does von Paulus think?"

Jodl pursed his lips carefully. He had already guessed that von Paulus was trying to use the defection, if that was what it was, of Wotan to show just how low the morale of his command was. It would he an excuse for another attempt to persuade the Führer to let him withdraw. Personally, he didn't like the idea for two reasons. One, von Paulus wouldn't make it, in his opinion. Two, he thought that to sacrifice von Paulus and his army at Stalingrad would act as an inspiration to the rest of the *Wehrmacht*. The tide was turning against Germany. The *Wehrmacht* needed the example of an army which fought to the last man and the last bullet. "He thinks the Regiment has deserted, *mein Führer*," Jodl answered Hitler's question.

"*Deserted*!" Hitler echoed aghast.

Himmler, his sallow weak face flushing suddenly, said in that high-pitched voice of his, "Impossible. The SS does not desert, especially my Wotan. I would vouch for that regiment with my life."

Jodl looked from one man to the other. They were both dilettantes, who had managed to condemn a whole army to its doom. Now that things were falling apart, they didn't know what to do

"Well," Hitler snapped finally, "how *do* you explain their disappearance at this hour of crisis? More importantly, what are you going to do about it, *Reichsfuhrer*?"

Himmler winced visibly. The Führer was addressing him by rank not by his name, as he usually did. That was a sign of great disfavour. "I have to know more first, *mein Führer*," Himmler said, taking off his pince-nez and cleaning the glass nervously. "There is some explanation, I am sure of it, *mein Führer*!"

"And if there isn't?" Hitler demanded coldly.

"Well—"

"I shall tell you," Hitler interrupted as Himmler stuttered. "The Wotan column will be located and liquidated to the last man."

Even Jodl, the unflappable professional, was shocked. "You mean – wiped out, sir?"

"Yes. By air. Bomb them to pieces. If an elite SS unit runs away, what can I expect of my poor infantry of the *Wehrmacht* at Stalingrad. An example must be set to keep the others fighting."

Jodl nodded his understanding. At least, Hitler had made no mention of evacuating the Sixth Army from Stalingrad. It would die there and the legend would be born.

Hitler looked hard at Himmler, "*Reichsfuhrer*, you are dismissed. You can set about getting to the bottom of this nasty business at once. We don't want the rot to spread."

Himmler roused himself from his shocked stupor like a man fighting to awake from a deep sleep. "*Jawohl, mein Führer*," he said miserably. He raised his right arm in the 'German greeting' and said, "Heil Hitler!"

The Führer didn't seem even to notice. Instead he turned to Jodl and barked, "*Herr Generaloberst*, please brief me on this business of awarding von Paulus the oak leaves to his Knight's Cross. It could give him a bit more backbone and steadfastness."

"Well, sir, if we do that, it will be sign that you have the fullest confidence in him. That, I am sure, will increase von Paulus' staying power—"

Effectively cut off from the conversation, Himmler slunk out miserably, telling himself he was in disgrace and if that were not to be a permanent state of affairs, he'd have to do something about Geier and his damned Wotan fast.

He had no eyes for the streets of Berlin, as his chauffeur drove the big black Horch through the afternoon traffic, the black-uniformed SS captain driver hitting his horn every time someone seemed about to get in his way. Berlin was beflagged as usual and there were patriotic slogans everywhere: "*Wheels Roll For Victory*" . . . "*Victory for Siberia*". But the civilians returning from work with their shabby imitation briefcases in which they had carried their sandwiches, looked pale and undernourished.

Himmler saw none of this. He was too preoccupied with his own problems and by the time he reached his own office, he was thoroughly depressed. He knew he should start making enquiries about the missing SS formation at once. But he hadn't the strength. It was as if someone had opened a tap and all the energy had drained from his frail body.

Bertha, his secretary-mistress, sensed at once that something was wrong as he came through the door and took off his black cap with its proud skull-and-crossbones badge. She glanced through the window to see if they were being observed. Then when she saw they weren't, she blew him a kiss and said, "You look all in, Heini, would you like a peppermint tea? You know how that always perks you up."

He shook his head as he slumped down in the chair opposite Bertha, who was plump and homely, wore spectacles and sensible shoes as befitted German women, for whom Himmler had decreed, 'A German woman does not smoke or redden her lips.' "Something stronger, if you please, my little cheetah. I've had a dreadful five minutes with the Führer."

She tut-tutted. But obedient German woman as she was who did not 'smoke or redden her lips', she walked across to the cupboard which contained the bottle of kirsch liqueur which they allowed themselves on that evening, once a month, when Heini had the strength to be intimate with her. She poured him a careful tot and then one for herself, too.

"*Prost*," Himmler said moodily, raising the little glass.

"*Prost*," she answered, coming over to run her fingers (devoid of nail polish naturally) through his thinning hair. "You know, Heini, it's still two weeks before we can do

– you know what again." She lowered her gaze demurely and fluttered her eyebrows.

"I know, *Liebste*," he agreed. "But I need something to cheer me up."

"What happened?" she asked carefully balancing her considerable weight on his skinny knees.

"One of my regiments has seemingly deserted on the Eastern Front. Our beloved Führer has ordered me to do something very drastic about it. But the very thought of hurting my own SS men makes me almost physically sick."

"Poor Heini," she pressed his hand lovingly, tears sparkling behind her glasses. "What a tremendous weight you have to bear in this dreadful war." She made up her mind. "Then you shall be spoiled this afternoon. You certainly deserve to be spoiled. After that, you can make your decision."

He flashed her a thin smile. "Thank you my beloved. Will it be everything?" he added hopefully.

"Everything," she promised, taking off her glasses as she drained the rest of the *Kirsch* in one gulp.

"Including the lash?" he ventured, astomished at his own temerity.

"*The lash*," she said, her voice suddenly much deeper and very threatening. "You have been naughty. The Führer himself has said so. Now you must be punished, my boy." She looked at him very fiercely. "Now I shall go and prepare myself in our sleeping quarters. It will take me some time. But you must contain yourself – and woe betide you if you can't. I will not have you fumbling with yourself. Is that understood?"

"Yes, mistress," he said humbly, heart beating wildly as he already visualized the pains and pleasures that lay ahead for him.

"Good, on my command you will knock and enter. Thereupon, you will confess your sins. Do you understand?"

"Yes," he quavered.

"Good. I am glad you realise that it will be no use trying to hide anything from me. It will only increase your punishment – and punished you must be."

"I understand that," he answered, voice thick and shaky.

"*Severely* punished!" Her voice was an octave lower. "Severely."

"Yes mistress."

"Now I must go." Her ample bottom swaying firmly from side to side, she strode determined into the study-cum-bedroom, while he sat there trembling, wondering if he dare have another *Kirsch*. She didn't like him to have another *Kirsch*. Finally after some minutes, he decided he needed the courage the alcohol would give him. But hardly had he reached for the bottle, when her voice commanded harshly. "In here, slave. At once . . . or it will be the worse for you, you miserable little worm."

The master of millions of slaves, the head of the world's most hated military formation, the SS, the most feared man in Europe put down his little glass as if it were red-hot. "I'm coming, my mistress," he gulped, his lips suddenly very dry as he heard the crack of her whip. "At once . . . at once."

"By God, hurry it up," she threatened from within, "or I'll wrap the lash around that skinny rump of yours till you scream with absolute pain."

"I'm coming," he quavered, "Honestly, I'm coming . . ."

Chapter Nine

"Oh, Heini, how masterful you were!" Bertha gushed when he came back into the office dressed now, his wounds soothed with powder. "What power you possess, darling."

He nodded stiffly and told himself he'd better keep on standing; his backside was too tender. He did feel better – and, what was more important, in charge."

She had received him with the shutters drawn and with a single red light glowing on the bedside table. She had been transformed. Gone was the drab business suit, the sensible shoes, the spectacles. Now she had worn a transparent black silk gown which had revealed all her fleshy nakedness. Her legs had been encased in high-heeled black leather boots which came to her plump thighs, and in her hands she had carried a thin, cruel-looking riding crop. He had begun to tremble violently as soon as he had seen it, knowing what was to come.

"Well, slave," she had commanded in a deep threatening bass, "what are you waiting for? Get them off. Quick! Or it will be the worse for you." She had slapped her palm with the riding crop and had made him jump.

Hurriedly he had torn off his uniform, gazing at her in hungry, fearful anticipation. She had watched him, slapping the riding crop against her hand back and forth, over and over again like a clock ticking off the seconds before the punishment would commence.

She had looked him up and down when he had finished, taking in his skinny shanks and concave, hairless chest. "Is that all you have to bring your mistress, you idle wretch?" she had demanded contemptuously. With her crop she had lifted his limp flaccid penis. "How can you pleasure me, blister my insides, with that piece of worthless gristle?" She had given it a playful tap with the crop and he had jumped with pain.

"I'm sorry," he had quavered abjectly.

"You're always sorry," she had snapped harshly. "Always excuses. Well, my dear sir, I fear there is no excuse this time. You will have to pay the price for your failings. Down on all fours – *at once!*"

"Must I?" he had asked, voice a mixture of fear and sexual anticipation.

"You are absolutely shameless. Not another word from you. How dare you query your mistress. *On all fours!*" She cracked the whip threateningly.

He had knelt hurriedly, heart beating furiously.

"Thrust up that disgusting rump of yours," she commanded. *"Wirds bald?"*

He responded immediately, thrusting up his skinny yellow buttocks. "Don't be too hard on me," he pleaded in a strange far-away little voice, "please."

She laughed harshly. "You will get what you deserve, you disgusting wretch." Next moment, the crop came down hard across his rump, so hard that he could not hold back the sob of joy and pain. Then she began to belabour him with all her might, face crimson and lathered in sweat as she did so. And he writhed and twisted, crying all the time, "Stop . . . oh, please don't stop . . . *STOP!*"

Ten minutes later with his backside red and bleeding, he had taken her quite savagely for him, and she had gasped with pleasure, clutching him to her wet, naked body, crying time and time again, "Oh, how good you are to me, Heini!"

Now, as he stood there, hurting, but in full control of the situation, no longer afraid of the Führer's anger, he said, "My dear, get me the squadron commander of the Black Hawks."

"*Hauptsturmfuhrer* Boldt?"

"Yes," he said very businesslike, already rehearsing what he would say to the young SS flier.

A few moments later she had the commander of the SS's own air squadron on the phone. The squadron was based close to the old Polish-Russian frontier, but the connection was as clear as if Boldt were in the next room.

"Boldt," he said without preliminaries, "*Reichsfuhrer* SS. I have a mission for you – priority number one, Boldt."

"*Reichsfuhrer*." There was instant respect in the voice at other end, a thousand kilometres away. Himmler liked the sound. He flashed Bertha a confident smile. He was in charge now and he knew it. "It will be your task to locate SS Assault Regiment Wotan, which has deserted the Stalingrad front—"

"Wotan," Boldt interrupted, the shock in his voice quite clear, "But Colonel Geier's Wotan—"

"Listen and don't talk, Boldt," Himmler said firmly.

"Wotan is to be located. Once you have done so, report to me immediately and I shall give the order to wipe them out. Every last one of the traitors, a disgrace to the SS, will be liquidated. Is that clear, Boldt?"

"Yes, *Reichsfuhrer*."

"I expect an identification and report within the next twelve hours. This is a matter of utmost importance. Get to it, *Ende*." He slammed the phone down and looked triumphantly at Bertha who cooed, impressed.

"Oh, Heini, how well you handled that. I really do think we should do," she lowered her eyes demurely for a moment, "*it* twice a month. It's so good for you."

"Certainly, if affairs of state will allow it, Bertha," Himmler said. "Now then, about that lance-corporal in the "Death's Head" who asked for permission to marry a woman whose great-great-grandfather apparently had some Polish blood in him."

Obediently Bertha picked up her secretary's pad. Heini, she told herself as her lover began to dictate, was constantly burdened by these high-level decisions. It must be very hard for him. "The highest degree of racial purity in the SS is," Himmler was saying . . .

A thousand kilometres away, *Hauptsturmfuhrer* Boldt swung his highly polished riding boots onto the battered desk and frowned at the snowflakes falling outside. Adolf Boldt, tall, lean and absolutely ruthless normally, was shocked by Himmler's order. In 1939 he had been a member of Wotan himself. Then he had volunteered to become an aerial artillery observer, which had led to his being given command of the *Waffen SS*'s only air squadron, which Himmler had ordered to be formed in 1941 after a row with Air Marshal Goering, head of the *Luft-waffe*. With its obsolete Stuka dive-bombers, the 'Black Hawks' as they were called, usually helped to blast the way forward for the *Waffen SS*'s armoured divisions. Now apparently they were expected to destroy one of those same formations.

Boldt rose to his feet and looked at his handsome face in the steel shaving mirror nailed to the office wall. He often did this when he wanted to see if his face revealed any hidden doubts. Now he could see it did. How could he undertake an active operation against officers like the Vulture or von Dodenburg who had once been his comrades? Yet at the same time he was under orders to do so, and he had no doubt what would happen to him, if he refused. His own life would be on the line. "Old house," he said softly, to his own image, "they've got you with your balls between the anvil and the hammer on this one." It was true. Either solution would be wrong.

"Let's take it one step at a time," he told his reflection. "That's the only way. Find Wotan first – and not too fast at that – and then make the decision about what is to be done. Perhaps, if it takes long enough, everything will have been cleared up." He nodded his agreement with his image.

A moment later, he crossed to the door and pulled his black leather flying jacket from the nail, following it with his battered cap, which he tilted at a rakish angle. Finally, he slung a white silk scarf carelessly around the black and white enamel of the Knight's Cross which dangled from his neck. Pleased that he looked every inch the typical devil-may-care-pilot he strode out into the whirling snow, whistling jauntily, as if he hadn't a care in the world.

The pilots' mess was like every other mess he had ever seen. Pilots in various stages of undress of uniform were clustered around the battered piano singing their hearts out. Others sprawled out in cracked leather chairs were sucking on their pipes and reading old illustrated magazines, usually pornographic.

Boldt told himself he must have been in scores of such places. They were all so standard: the chamber pots lined up on the window sills which were sometimes used for drinking wagers; the sign stolen from the State Railway which proclaimed, *"It is strictly forbidden to use the latrine when the train is stationary"*; and everywhere of course, bits and pieces of shotdown planes – there was even a prop from a crashed Tommy Spitfire.

The pilots were the same, too. Young, handsome and somehow elegant even in undress uniform. They all had the usual tokens and mascots. Count von Polski never flew without a teddy bear next to him. Bruno von und zu Pulitz owned an ancient Mercedes tourer in which he raced around in pursuit of female conquests, invariably returning the following morning with a pair of knickers fluttering from the radio aerial. Prince Metternich indulged himself in a baby tiger, with which he was often photographed for the illustrated magazines.

But Boldt knew that these sons of the penniless Bavarian-Austrian aristocracy had not joined the SS because they were fervent National Socialists. They weren't. They had joined because the SS was a means for retrieving their lost fortunes. Himmler had been born at the old royal Bavarian court. He worshipped the aristocracy, and all of them knew that through him the SS Stuka Squadron, the Black Hawks, was their chance to regain their old pre-1918 importance. None of them would hesitate a minute if it came to a test between their loyalty to the SS and securing their future. The future came first.

"Gentlemen," Boldt announced as he closed the door behind him, "let's have some silence in the knocking shop. We have a mission."

Thirty minutes later they were on their way, with Boldt praying the snowstorm would go on for ever.

Chapter Ten

"I was once with a pavement pounder who had an arrow tattoed above her muff," Matz said thoughtfully, as he and Schulze crouched in the shelter of the ruined *Isba*, trying to keep out of the snow-laden wind.

"Why was that?" Schulze asked without much interest, as he spooned "old man", meat reputedly made from the bodies of old men from Berlin's workhouses, out of a tin. "No, on second thoughts, don't tell me. It was there for birdbrains like you to know where the slit was."

The answer didn't offend Matz one little bit. "Well, how do you explain then, arse-with-ears, that she had a mouse tattoed on her butt?" he asked.

"I give up," Schulze said, finishing off the cold meat and tossing the tin away carelessly. "Why?"

Matz, his nose red and dripping with the cold looked at his old comrade triumphantly and said, "I don't know. It's the same as with the arrow."

Schulze shook his head like a man sorely tried, but said nothing. It was too much of an effort . . .

They had been moving for twenty-four hours now. Progress had been slow but smooth. The centre of the Pocket through which they were moving seemed to be almost devoid of German troops, and so far they had not encountered any of the enemy partisans who were said to be operating now inside the German positions.

It was almost as if they were passing through a world at peace, virtually devoid of human beings. Indeed, only the muted thunder of the guns to the east reminded them that the battle of Stalingrad was reaching its climax.

As the Vulture said to von Dodenburg, ten metres away from where the two NCOs huddled against the ruined hut, "We've been damned lucky so far von Dodenburg. But our luck won't last unless we make it ourselves. Our own people will have discovered by now that we – er – have made a withdrawal – and will have reported it to the authorities. Undoubtedly, they will act, probably drastically. It won't be too good for the morale of the rest of the Sixth Army if they let us get away with it."

Von Dodenburg looked worried, "My God, sir, I hope it doesn't come to that!"

"It will, if they catch us now before we reach von Manstein. But if we bring out Wotan virtually intact, then we have a good chance. Remember, they had a German general shot last summer in the Caucasus for withdrawing without orders. He was shot because he didn't pull it off. So, my dear fellow, our first priority is to save our own skins. It's as simple as that." He chuckled, but there was no warmth in the sound. "With a bit of luck, we'll reach the breakout point without interference. Then I'm afraid we'll have to deal with our own people and *then* the Russians."

"I don't like it, sir," replied von Dodenburg, as the snow came down in a steady stream and the men stamped up and down in the white gloom trying to bring some life into their leaden feet.

"You're not expected to, von Dodenburg. You're with us. You'll swing with the rest of us if things go wrong –" he stopped short. "What's that?" he barked, cocking his head to the wind and removing his thick ear muffs.

Von Dodenburg turned his head, too. Now he heard it.

A long doleful howling which set the small hairs at the back of his head standing erect. "Wolves?" he queried.

The Vulture shook his head. "I don't think so. In this part of Russia they don't have – *Look*!" He pointed excitedly.

A small, dark shape had emerged from the whirling storm. It stopped and raising its ugly snout, sniffed the air.

"That's a dog," the Vulture said.

"Yes, you're right, sir. And what's that on its back?" Von Dodenburg narrowed his eyes to slits and peering through the snow, tried to make out the object strapped to the lone dog's back.

Matz, who had the keenest eyesight in the whole of Wotan, was quicker off the mark. "Battle dog!" he yelled, springing to his feet, the hinges of his wooden leg creaking as he did so. *"Popov battle dog."*

Next to him, still sitting, Schulze unslung his machine pistol, as the shout alarmed the dog, which now started to trot forward to the nearest armoured vehicle. He snatched at the trigger. A burst of tracer zapped towards the dog. The burst fell short. Little spurts of snow sprang up in a line ten metres to its front.

The dog reacted immediately. Its ears down flat the length of its sloping skull, it broke to the left and pelted towards a lone Tiger, the crew of which were invisible, probably sheltering inside the metal monster from the storm, so they did not see the battle dog.

Furiously Schulze fired off another burst and more and more of the grenadiers joined in trying to hit the dog before it reached its target. But the Russian animal seemed to bear a charmed life. Now it was almost there, the little aerial attached to the high explosive strapped to its back flipping back and forth as it ran all out.

"Christ on a crutch!" Matz wailed impotently. "Somebody hit the shitting thing before it's too late –" The rest of his words were drowned by a thick crump of explosive, as the dog dived beneath the tank, the aerial striking one of the bogies and detonating the high explosive.

Bloody chunks of the dead animal flew everywhere, as the tank's track snapped, trailing out behind it like a broken limb, with the bogies on the Tiger's left side still going, so that the sixty ton fighting vehicle slumped to one side, thick black smoke already streaming from its great ruptured engine. A second later the fuel tanks exploded. In an instant, the Tiger was wreathed in flame, one crew member hanging dying in the turret, his head wreathed in blue fire, while the driver twisted and turned in the snow, screaming hysterically, as the flames consumed him.

Now the battle dogs were streaming out of the white gloom on all sides, heading straight for the armour. They had been trained by their handlers to head straight for the smell of oil and steel, running towards their death, as the Wotan troopers rallied and poured volley after volley at the approaching animals.

Then as abruptly as it had started, the strange, unexpected attack ceased, leaving behind a loud, echoing silence, broken only by the hiss of the flames on the shattered tank and the pitiful whimpering of a dying dog.

The Vulture wiped the sweat from his strained face. "Well, there you have it," he announced.

Von Dodenburg nodded.

Creeping Jesus looked from one face to the other in bewilderment. "What . . . have what?" he asked.

Von Dodenburg looked down at his narrow, mean face disdainfully. "If you'd have spent more time at the front, you would have known. Partisans! Even partisans use battle dogs. Apart from Molotov cocktails, they are the only kind of anti-tank weapons they possess."

"So," the Vulture summed up for the adjutant grimly, "it means that the partisans are on to us. We've been spotted. Now the question is if they will alert their regular troops that a German armoured regiment is moving around inside the Pocket. If they do, we can expect trouble long before we reach our start line for the breakout. All right, Adjutant, get to work. We'll roll again. Better to keep moving as much as we can now, especially under the cover of this snowstorm."

"Sir." Creeping Jesus doubled away clumsily through the ankle-deep snow to alert the tank crews, as the Vulture turned to face his second-in-command. "Von Dodenburg, I am putting you in charge of anti-partisan ops. Take a company of panzer grenadiers in half-tracks. You'll provide protection to both our flanks to a depth of half a kilometre each way. Keep radio traffic down to a minimum. I don't want the Ivans – our own people for that matter – to be able to pinpoint our positions through the radiowaves."

Von Dodenburg nodded his understanding. "You will lead the armour, sir?"

"Exactly. We shall link up again just east of Kalnach. In this kind of weather, I imagine it'll take twenty-four hours to reach that place, and if I were a religious man, which I'm not, I would be praying hard by now that we don't lose any more Tiger tanks, and that the Russians, who are usually slow to react, don't attack us again before we reach our startline for the breakout. Well, that's it, von Dodenburg. *Hals und Beinbruck.*"*

* Literally "Break your neck and legs", ie. happy landings.

Von Dodenburg clicked to attention. "Thank you, sir. The same to you." He saluted. Then, turning, he shouted, "All right, Sergeant Schulze, stop feeding your ugly mug. I've got a job for you."

Schulze moaned, "Ain't there ever going to be any peace for a poor old broken-down stubble-hopper?" But he came doubling over readily enough, for he was devoted to the handsome blond major, who, fanatical as he was, wouldn't waste his men's lives in the same manner that the Vulture would if necessary. He snapped to attention, "Sergeant Schulze," he barked with mock formality, "reporting as ordered."

"Stick it up yer ass!" von Dodenburg said, knowing Schulze of old. The big Hamburger had no respect for officers or the formalities of service regulations. "Get over to Hauptsturm Giskes and tell him to have his company saddled up and ready to go in ten minutes. Take Matz with you. We're off on flank guard."

Schulze crossed himself with a saintly look on his red face, or as saintly as that tough, ugly mug could ever produce, and intoned solemnly, "For what we are about to receive, let the Good Lord make us truly thankful."

Von Dodenburg raised his clenched fist threateningly.

Schulze fled . . .

Half a kilometre away, Boldt caught a brief glimpse of cherry red flame through the gap in the snowstorm. It was the burning Tiger, though he didn't know it at that moment. He did know, however, that there were no German troops in this particular part of the Pocket. He put his fingers to his throat mike to report his sighting. Then thought better of it. "Give the poor shits, if they are down there, a chance," he said to himself in the manner of lonely men. "For a little while longer." Then he banked away and the fire vanished back into the snowstorm. For the time being, SS Asault Regiment Wotan was safe. *But for how long?*

PART TWO

Breakout

"He who fights and runs away, lives to fight another day".

Old Military Edict

Chapter One

Visibility was virtually nil. The wind howled down the narrow country track, leading to the huddle of straw-roofed huts. It whipped up the new snow in a frenzied dance. The snow penetrated every gap in the waiting men's uniforms, lashing their frozen, crimson faces, clinging to their boots in huge clumps.

But blanketed as they were in their icy cocoons of vicious white, the panzer grenadiers were glad of the cover the snowfall provided. By now they knew the miserable Russian village was occupied – they could smell the sweet smell of logs that burned in the ceiling-high ovens which heated the *isbas*. But whether by Germans or Russians, they didn't know.

"What about it, sir?" Schulze asked finally. "Do we have a look-see? Sooner or later they'll tumble to us being out here and my appendages—"

"Your what?" von Dodenburg interrupted.

"My balls. You being an officer and a gentlemen, I didn't want to use a crude word to you, sir. You might have been offended." Schulze grinned.

"Get on with it, you big rogue."

"So let's get on with it before my balls freeze up totally, sir."

"Mine, too. All right, Schulze." Von Dodenburg made his decision. "Take a dozen men. Post two of them at each of the two exits and then go in with the rest. But be careful. I want no casualties if I can help it."

"Don't worry, sir. Whoever's in there will have to get up a lot earlier if he wants to catch Frau Schulze's handsome son with his knickers down." Suddenly he was very businesslike. "All right, you Matz. You, too, One Flipper. You . . . and you. *Mir nach*." With surprising swiftness for such a big man, he was up and was moving down the track almost before the others had had time to unsling their weapons and follow.

Anxiously von Dodenburg watched until they disappeared into the snowstorm. Then he turned and stamped his way back a couple of hundred metres to where the halftracks, packed with freezing, shivering panzer grenadiers waited. "Signaller," he snapped to his radioman. "Signal Sunray," he used the Vulture's code-name. "Bumped into occupied village. Reccing it."

"Sir."

"High speed morse. Nice and fast. Don't want to give our position away."

Immediately the signaller bent to his task, while von Dodenburg waited, smoking pensively, wondering how his two rogues were getting on in the village.

Schulze, followed at two metres by Matz, advanced carefully towards the collection of huts huddled around an onion-topped church that looked as if it hadn't seen a service these many years; but then Schulze told himself that communists had banned religion in the '20's. Now they knew the village was definitely occupied. They could hear faint noises from within the huts, and the outer walls, where the oven was, felt warm to the touch, indicating they were being used.

Schulze stopped and sniffed the air like a wild dog might. There, mingled with the smell of woodsmoke, was the stink of black *marhokka* tobacco, which only a Russian could bear to smoke – it was so horrible. Over his shoulder he whispered to Matz, "Popovs."

Matz tightened his grip on his bayonet, while Schulze hurriedly slipped on his 'Hamburg Equalizer', a fearsome pair of brass knuckles, with which he had won many a fight on Hamburg's waterfront before the war.

Schulze hesitated. He guessed that the Russians weren't from the Red Army; they would have posted sentries and the like. But were these just ordinary peasants, of whom there were a lot inside the Pocket, or were they partisans? They could even be both, as they often were, posing as simple peasants during the daylight hours and sallying forth as partisans at night.

Matz seemed able to read his thoughts, for he whispered urgently, "There's only one way to find out, Schulze. Let's get in there."

Schulze nodded. "All right," he hissed, "on a count of three then." *"One . . . two . . . three."* With one mighty kick, Schulze smashed the door open.

A woman shrieked. An old man with a wispy white beard, sleeping on the shelf that formed a bed right round the oven fell over in alarm, while another grabbed an axe and raised it threateningly. But when he saw the crimson-faced giant at the door with the brass knuckles gleaming on a hamlike fist, he thought better of it and dropped it as if the handle had suddenly become red hot.

Matz and Schulze flashed a quick look around the poverty-stricken place. There were no weapons in sight and all of the occupants were too old to be in the partisans. "So poor they haven't even got a pot to piss," Matz commented.

"*Sto?*" the old crone finally quavered, still holding the

hem of her long, dirty white skirt to her withered lips with fright.

"*Germanski*," Schulze managed to force a smile to reassure her. "*Gdre partisani?*"

The old man on the hard-baked clay floor shook his head. "*Nix partisani*," he croaked.

Schulze sucked his bottom lip. He thought that these people were too frightened to lie. But he knew the Russians by now. They were a devious people. After all, most of their history they had been forced to lie to Tartars, Czars, communists in order to save their own skins. "Matz," he decided finally, "just keep an eye on 'em. I'll check the next *isba*. *Ponemyu?*"

"*Ponmyu*," Matz answered also in his pidgen Russian, for like all the old hares who seemed to have been in Russia for ever, he salted his speech with bits of Russian.

Schulze went out. In the white gloom he could see the rest of the men approaching the *isbas*. He told himself they could take care of the huts; he'd have a look at the rundown church, the stucco paint long peeled off its walls, leaving them ugly and scarred like the symptoms of some loathsome skin disease.

It was occupied. He could hear a faint murmur of voices coming from within it, and surprisingly, for as Matz had remarked, the peasants were too poor even to have "a pot to piss in", there was the definite smell of roasting fresh meat, too. Schulze licked his lips as if in anticipation. He went through the door.

The nave of the church was packed with drunken soldiers grouped around a huge bonfire obviously of floorboards from the abandoned church on which two men were turning a small pig on a makeshift spit, the fat dripping from it and spluttering in the flames.

For a moment a dumbfounded Schulze stared at the

drunken soldiers who so far had not seen him as he crouched there in the aisle. They were German soldiers all right. But there was something strange about them. Then he spotted it. The German eagle with the swastika underneath had been removed from their tunics, as had their epaulettes. And those who still wore caps had turned them, for some strange reason, inside out with the lining on the outside.

"Great crap on the Christmas tree," he muttered to himself, "what in three devils' name is going on here?"

Then he remembered what his father, "Broken Nose" Schulze, one of the waterfront's greatest bare-knuckle fighters, had told him of the 1910 mutiny of the Imperial Fleet and Army in Hamburg in 1918. "Yer see, son, the hairy-assed front swine didn't want to be associated with the old Imperial Army. They'd mutinied, but they had nothing else to wear but their uniforms. So they tore off their badges, epaulettes and the like, and turned their caps inside out to show the world they didn't belong to the Kaiser's troops no more. "Then he added," Now I've gone and talked mesen dry, son. Go and fetch me a jug o' suds from Hansen's *Krug*. Be a good lad. And don't go talking to Fat Erna, the whore, on yer way. I'm sure she's been putting nasty ideas into yer noddle. Playing with it agen last night you was. It'll fall off if you keep that up, yer know." And with that dread warning still ringing in his youthful easy, Schulze had sped off to the waterfront drinking hole at the corner, to get the old man his 'suds'.

Now he saw it all. This mob had decided they'd had enough of the Hell of Stalingrad and were showing it publicly. But what the sod were they going to do, he asked himself. They were still in the Pocket. Where were they thinking of going?

Suddenly a soldier fastening up his flies and remarking that "it's colder than a witch's tit out yonder" came up the aisle. He stopped short when he saw the giant crouching there, with the "Hamburg Equalizer" on his hand and the machine pistol slung across his broad back. "Hey," he snarled, "who are you when yer at home, *Kumpel*?"*

"I'm no frigging *Kumpel* of yourn," Schulze said boldly. "Who *are* you when *you're* at frigging home, eh?"

The soldier stuck a thumb at his skinny chest and said, "I'm asking the frigging questions 'cos there's more of us. Hey, men," he raised his voice so that he could be heard above the drunken racket. "We've got a spy here, Looks like frigging SS to me."

The drunken mutineers turned startled, some of them holding bottles of looted vodka to their lips, others holding bayonets at the ready to carve off a piece of the sizzling pork, once the pig was done. An excited mutter of voices broke out. "What yer doing here?" some demanded. Others cried, "Are you with us or agen us, you SS bastard?" A couple cried, "Shoot the big shit here and now. They'd do the same to us!"

Schulze felt his mind racing electrically. These were desperate men, he realised that. The front swine all lived short, brutal lives. Now they had deserted, their lives were doomed to be even shorter if they were caught. They wouldn't hesitate a moment to kill anyone who got in their way. Hurriedly he held up his hand for peace, while he prayed that outside, Matz or one of the others had tumbled to what was going on. Now he spoke, raising his voice so that outside they might just

---

* *Kumpel*, universal form of address among German soldiers. Roughly "mate".

hear him, "Look comrades, we're in the same boat as you are. We're doing a bunk as you are. We're out to save our skins as well."

They looked at him suspiciously. One of them, an evil-looking, cross-eyed fellow with a sallow, pock-marked skin, asked, "What, just a handful of yer? Or perhaps a whole nunch, complete with officers and gents?" He looked around him at his comrades knowingly, seeing they had got his point.

Some of the mutineers nodded sagely. Others said, "Come on, croak the SS swine and let's get it over with. My guts are doing flip-flops with hunger."

"We've got officers with us. But they're just like us," Schulze answered reluctantly. "They're on the trot as well."

"Don't believe one frigging word he sez," the cross-eyed man warned.

Abruptly, a voice, harsh, incisive and obviously used to giving orders and having them obeyed – snapped, "Enough of that. This man might be of use to us."

The noise died away almost immediately, as a tall man, one side of his face distorted with sabre scars, pushed his way through the crowd and faced Schulze. He was as tall as Schulze, but leaner, much leaner, and those scars from his days as a student duellist and his haughty bearing marked him obviously as an ex-officer. Now he snapped, "What's your unit, *Overscharfuhrer*?"

"SS Assault Regiment Wotan, sir."

"No 'sirs'. We're all equal here." The man stroked his clean-shaven chin, the only one in the whole nave. "I've heard of your outfit. The elite of the elite. If Wotan is running away, then the whole Pocket is collapsing. That is indeed interesting information for our – er – friends. All right," he made a decision, "take him to that little room behind the altar. Lock him up there till we have time to question—"

Schulze lashed out suddenly with the Hamburg Equalizer. But he was just a shade too slow. The cross-eyed man had crept up behind him. Now the cruelly brass-shod butt of his rifle crashed down at the back of Schulze's neck. Schulze bellowed, went down on his knees, hands flailing the air as if trying to keep upright. In vain. Next moment, he pitched forward, unconscious before he hit the hard stone floor.

Outside the church, Matz hesitated. His every instinct was for going in there, machine pistol blazing. But his reason told him that wouldn't do his old running mate much good. He guessed there were too many of them. He'd have to get back to the Chief. Von Dodenburg would know what to do. He waved to the others then they began to withdraw from the village like thieves in the night . . .

Chapter Two

Automatically Boldt stood to attention at the phone, while all around him in the "ready-room", his aristocratic pilots sprawled full length in the battered chairs, leafing idly through week-old magazines or looking arrogantly amused at their commander, who was obviously receiving a 'rocket' from Reichsfuhrer SS Himler.

"We've damned well got to find Wotan soon. The Führer is breathing down my neck already and 'Fat Hermann'," he meant Hermann Goering, the enormously fat head of the German *Luftwaffe*, "is offering to supply planes for the search, although he can't even keep up the re-supply of Stalingrad. Now another half battalion of Seydlitz-Kurzbach's 94th Infantry Division have deserted. Apparently they shot some of their officers and senior NCOs who wouldn't go with them. But the rest did. The rot is spreading fast, Boldt. The Führer said that himself. He wants to set an example of Wotan – and quick!"

"I understand sir, fully," Boldt answered swiftly, as the skinny *Reichsfuhrer* paused for breath. "But up here the weather conditions are frightful. The runway's like glass. Then as soon as we clear it with the burner, the damp freezes over again. Visibility is down to ten metres. Once we're airborne, we're virtually sightless."

"Drop flares," Himmler suggested.

"We've tried, *Reichsfuhrer*. But even the most powerful won't penetrate that pea-soup."

"Well, they must be found and I tell you there will be a reward for the first pilot to spot them. None of your usual tin." He meant decorations and medals. "I know your chaps have got a chestful of that sort of stuff already. But what about three days' leave in Paris, with all the champus and women the chap desires – at my expense?" Now his voice, which had warmed for a moment, became harsh and oppressive once more. "There is no more time to be lost. Find them. *Ende.*" The line went dead.

"The usual rocket?" asked Baron Karst, who affected a monocle and riding crop, and flew wearing cavalry breeches as if he were back in the days of Richthofen's Flying Circus. "The Reichsheini's voice sounded somewhat strident."

"The usual rocket."

Karst shrugged casually. "We can't do wonders – he should know that."

Boldt grunted something and stared gloomily at the pair of black silk knickers, decorated with red lace, which von und zu Pulitz had hung on the notice board after returning from one of his nightly amorous missions. Under it was printed the legend, "SHOT DOWN IN THREE MINUTES FLAT".

"He said there would be a reward for the first man to spot Wotan," he said, breaking his silence after a few minutes.

"A reward," someone snorted. "Not another of those pieces of tin which the Führer keeps dreaming up? I've already cured my throatache, won the scrambled egg and have been honoured with the frozen meat order." He meant the Knight's Cross, the German Cross in Gold and the Frostbite Medal. "Dearie me, I'd have my monthlies if I won another bit of that junk."

He made a great show of moping his brow with a floral silk handkerchief as if the very thought caused him great distress.

"No, not another piece of tin," Boldt said. "Three days in Paris with wine, women and song."

They sat up and Count von Polski actually dropped his beloved teddy bear mascot to chortle, "You mean Pig Alley, the Left Blank and all that Parisian ho-ha?"

"Exactly," Boldt said.

"But whose paying?" von und zu Pulitz said, making the continental gesture of counting notes with his thumb and forefinger.

"The Reichsfuhrer," Boldt answered, knowing that he was sealing the fate of his old unit, Wotan, by telling them this. Aristocrats, at least the ones he associated with in the Black Hawk Squadron, were completely unprincipled when it came to money. They'd do anything for it. That was the way their impoverished families had brought them up.

"What are we waiting for?" Karst asked excitedly. "I'd give my right nut for three days in Paris with *beaucoup* gash and buckets of champus."

"But the weather?" Boldt protested a little wearily. He knew already he was wasting his time. These pilots of his flew by the seat of their pants. The weather, however bad, had never worried the Black Hawks.

"The weather," von und zu Pulitz intoned, "can go and piss in its boot. Come on, chaps." There was a mad scramble for the door. Paris and all its decadent pleasures loomed ahead.

For a moment or two Boldt stayed in the room, listening to the crackle of the logs in the old iron stove in the corner, and the muted commands of the crew chiefs as they set about getting the Stukas ready for flight. Then he shook his head, as if trying to come out of a heavy sleep. There was nothing for it. He would have to join them in the search. Himmler would have his head if he didn't. He, personally, could do no more for SS Assault Regiment Wotan . . .

Boldt cruised at a steady one hundred kilometres an hour. Above the banks of green-glowing instruments, the perspex of the cockpit dripped rivulets of water. Forced through the cracks by the air pressure, the drops had fallen on to the knees of his flying overalls and stained them with dark damp stains. "Suppose I'll get rheumatism one of these days," he told himself idly, "if I live that long."

He came down lower, and trimmed the Stuka's speed to just above stalling level. The fog was as thick as ever and he wanted to take it as slowly as possible. Soon he would be crossing the River Karpovka, which was still held by the defenders of the Pocket. Beyond that, Boldt reasoned, Wotan would be swanning about. He tried, for a moment or two, to put himself in the Vulture's shoes. If the beak-nosed Colonel was tending to withdraw to von Manstein's Army, he'd want to keep that river between himself and the Ivans. So he must be heading in a generally south-westerly direction to where the tip of the Pocket was closest to von Manstein's forces. In other words he'd avoid contact with the Ivans as long as possible until he would be finally forced to fight his way out.

"The river, sir," the observer's muffled voice cut into his thoughts.

Boldt looked down. The fog had cleared a little and now they were flying down a kind of green avenue, the colour being reflected from the gloomy, massed firs down below. It was a little eerie, Boldt thought. It was as if they were flying down a murky cavern, lit by a funereal, unreal glow, heading straight for the broad stretch of water, which was the Karpovka.

"Something going on down there – to port, sir," the observer's voice filled his earphones. "Can you see?"

Boldt craned his neck. "Looks like bridging equipment. Must be the Ivans. Damn, I didn't think they'd got this far already." Boldt bit his bottom lip. Instinctively he flashed a glance into the rear-view mirror; it was something that he always did when something unexpected happened. It had saved his neck more than once.

"Shit on shingle!" he cursed and pulled back the stick, speeding up immediately. "To rear," he yelled to the observer. "Two . . . no, three Yak fighters!"

"Holy strawsack!" the observer cursed too, as angry blue lights rippled suddenly along the length of the first Yak's wings. Desperately he swung his single machine gun round to meet the challenge, as Boldt, sweating already, hurtled upwards, followed by angry red tracer like a flight of disturbed hornets.

The instinct of self-preservation returned in a flash. Suddenly he felt absolutely cool – in control of the situation. He smashed his foot down on the rudder bar. The Stuka howled in protest. Every rivet shrieked under the strain. Slugs pattered the length of its fuselage. There was the sound of rending to his rear. Abruptly the cockpit was full of the acrid stench of burnt explosive.

Behind Boldt, the observer yelled in triumph, as the Yak pilot caught by surprise by Boldt's sudden manoeuvre, flashed right above them, exposing his fat, khaki belly to the observer. Even in the fog, Boldt could see the angry blue sparks as the observer's bullets zipped the length of the Yak's belly. Metal rained down.

With sudden, totally unexpected startlingness, the Yak disintegrated in mid-air. The turbulence hit the Stuka as if it had just run into a solid brick wall. With all his strength, the sweat streaming down his face under the leather helmet, Boldt fought the Stuka as it bucked, juddered. For one agonising second, he thought the stick would be torn from his hands. And then he was in charge once more, and Boldt was hurtling for the cover of the deep fog a hundred metres away with the Yaks' tracer zipping after him, harmlessly.

"There'll be a piece of tin in this for you, Hartmann," he said to his observer as they reached the cover. "You did a shit-fine job just now."

"Do you think I could request an immediate transfer to the Pay Corps," the observer breathed over the intercom. "The brown stuff is still tricking down my left boot. Don't think I'm cut out for this sort of stuff."

Boldt grinned for a moment. Then his grin vanished as he realised what he had just seen. The Ivans were crossing the river in force. That had been large bridging equipment he had spotted minutes ago. And the crossing was important; otherwise the engineers wouldn't have had the aerial cover they had. But, he told himself, the most important thing of all was that there appeared to have been no German reaction from the Pocket. Where were the infantry who were supposed to be defending the far bank of the river?

Boldt pressed his throat mike. "Hartmann send this. To all. Break off the Wotan mission. Vital, return to base at once. Bomb up independently as soon as you touch down. *Ende.*" Grimly Boldt looked at his reflection in the perspex of the cockpit, illuminated by the green-glowing dials. For the time being, Wotan seemed to be saved, while they tackled this new threat. But the top brass wouldn't let Wotan get away with their withdrawal. Hitler and Himmler would want their pound of flesh sooner or later. Of that he was sure.

Chapter Three

Von Dodenburg listened attentively as an excited, worried Matz told his tale of what had happened in the village on the other side of the snowbound hill. He didn't interrupt the flow of words either until Matz explained how he had heard the man, who was obviously in charge, rasp, "This is interesting information for our – er – friends."

"Did he just say *friend*s, Corporal Matz?" he interjected.

"Yessir."

"Nothing else about who these *friends* might be?"

"Nosir. Then he just ordered that mob of mutineers to lock poor old Schulze up," Matz said, and fell silent for a moment.

Von Dodenburg sucked his bottom lip thoughtfully. What kind of friends would a couple of hundred mutineers have in the Pocket? And why were they sticking together? There were far too many of them in one heap. Normally, anyone who was on the trot did so on his own or with a friend. That way they didn't attract any attention from the dreaded chaindogs. And if they *were* picked up by the military police, well, then they could plead they had been cut off from their outfit and were trying to find their way back to it. That was always the standard excuse when deserters were picked up.

"Planes overhead!" One Flipper snapped urgently, breaking into von Dodenburg's reverie.

Everyone cocked their heads to the sky, eyes trying to penetrate the thick swirling fog.

Von Dodenburg licked suddenly-dry lips. If they were Germans and the pilots recognized the stalled halftracks as belonging to Wotan, which had withdrawn without orders, there'd be all hell to pay. He was quite sure the pilots would be ordered to attack them.

"They're not Ivan sewing machines," One Flipper said confidently. He meant the Soviet Rata reconnaissance planes which had a very distinctive engine noise – like that of an old-fashioned treadle sewing machine.

But as the seconds ticked by and the drone of the planes' engines started to draw away, they relaxed. Whatever they were – German or Russian – their pilots hadn't spotted the halftracks.

Von Dodenburg took up the conversation where they had left off. "How many of them were there, Matz?" he asked.

"Hard to say, sir. I didn't go inside, sir. But a lot. You could tell that by the racket they were kicking up. Lot of shitting sauce-hounds," he added bitterly, and then more urgently: "But what are we gonna do about Sergeant Schulze, sir? I know he's a pain in the frigging derriere most of the time – if you'll forgive my French – but he is my pal." He looked pleadingly at the officer.

"Don't wet yer drawers," von Dodenburg said, using one of Matz's own phrases in an attempt to reassure the little corporal. "You know what they say – weeds don't die that easily. We'll get the big rogue back one way or another." He left the worried corporal and strode over the frozen snow to the radio vehicle. "Signaller, get me the C.O." he ordered.

"Sir."

Hastily the signaller handed over the head-set to him. "Sunray," he snapped, knowing it was dangerous to speak in clear, terms but that it couldn't be avoided. Time was of the essence.

Almost instantly, the Vulture came on the air. "Sunray," he rasped.

"Sunray Two," von Dodenburg responded. In swift, clipped phrases, wasting absolutely no time on air, he told the Vulture what he had learned from Matz.

The Vulture listened attentively and then barked, "Your conclusion, Sunray Two?"

"Hard to say, save this:"

"What?"

"Those *friends*," von Dodenburg emphasized the word, "could well be the sons of Uncle Joe." He meant Josef Stalin, the Russian dictator.

Von Dodenburg could hear a surprised Vulture gasp on the other end. Then he said, "Understand. A piece of treachery to save their own cowardly hides!"

Von Dodenburg could have laughed out. Wasn't that exactly what they were doing too – trying to save their own cowardly hides? Instead he snapped, "Suggest I go and investigate. It might be to our advantage. Keep big friends," he meant Wotan's tanks, "ready to support us if necessary."

"Willdo. But to your advantage, Sunray Two?" the Vulture asked.

But von Dodenburg would talk no more. He could already hear the clicks in the radio as the Russian direction finders started to home in on his own radio. "*Ende*," he snapped hastily and handed the ear-phones back to the signaller.

He raised his voice. "All of you, listen to me. Five

men from each halftrack. There's something fishy about that village where they've got that big rogue, Sergeant Schulze." The men started to drop over the sides, weapons already being unslung for action. "The rest of you keep your eyes skinned—"

– "Like tinned tomatoes, sir, One Flipper said cheerfully. "You can rely on us old hares of Wotan."

Von Dodenburg knew he could, but it didn't do to get sloppy and sentimental with the "old hares", Wotan's veterans. So he said scornfully, "Rely on you shower o' shit? You lot'd rob yer own Fraulein mother blind. All right. *Los.* Let's go . . ."

In the little locked room behind the altar, that stank of rat droppings and incense, Sergeant Schulze brooded impatiently. It was over an hour now since they had captured him. Since that time nothing had happened save the men outside had got steadily drunker as they wolfed down the fat, half-charred lumps of pork – he could hear their grunts of pleasure and rough demands for "another piece, you greedy sod!" So, he concluded, the rest of his little recce party had gotten away safely and had by now reported what they had heard. He reasoned that an hour before, old Matz, legendary chowhound that he was, would have smelt that beautiful odour of roast pork right to the entrance of the abandoned church and heard what he had had to say to the mutineer with the scarred face

"They'll be coming back for you soon, old house. Don't worry Wotan never abandons its own." Of that he was confident. Now he was more concerned with what the drunks were up to. The ex-officer would be the one in the know, but how to get his paws on him before the balloon went up?

He rose from the little wooden bench on which he had been squatting and peered in the ruddy light coming in from outside the room. It was bare enough – the bench and some kind of three-legged prayer stool, like the kind they had been issued with when he had first joined the army as a recruit. Idly he picked it up by the hole in its centre. Back in 1938 they had marched to attention carrying those stools with them everywhere by the same kind of a grip. They used them as seats in lectures; supports for their rifles during musketry training. He stopped, the memories of that year so long ago suddenly forgotten. His big middle finger had come into contact with something sharp, protruding from the opening. He looked down and exclaimed, "Heaven, arse and cloudburst, a frigging nail!"

And he was right. A rusty nail had broken from the planks which made up the surface of the seat and penetrated into the grip. Schulze beamed down at it as if he had just discovered the Holy Grail. "As the whore said to the raw recruit, sonny, if you don't find the key, you won't open the door, and then she'd spread her pearly gates." He set to work at once . . .

Expertly, almost noiselessly the panzer grenadiers under von Dodenburg set about sealing off the old, onion-towered church. The straw roof of an abandoned *isba* facing the main door was pushed out. Minutes later a machine gun team was established there, legs astride the ancient beams. Anyone who tried to rush out of the church's door would be dead before he knew it. Troopers, with bags of grenades hanging from their shoulders, were positioned underneath the two great windows, both smashed and without glass. On a signal they could lob their stick grenades effortlessly through the open spaces. Other grenadiers, armed with picks and entrenching tools, were stationed to the rear in the dead ground. If necessary and if the mutineers inside the church decided to make a fight for it, they would "mousehole", which meant breaking through the wall and then into the next chamber, to take those inside by surprise. Within thirty minutes of arriving in the rundown village, von Dodenburg was sure that he had taken all appropriate measures and that his call for surrender, when it came, would be obeyed – or else.

Now he stood there in the snow, the mist swirling around his tall, lithe body, pistol in hand, waiting for the moment of decision – when he would start. For to judge from the racket coming from within the church, the mutineers were well and truly drunk and he didn't want some drunken private to blow out poor old Schulze's brains in a fit of trapped anger.

"Matz," he said.

"Sir," the little corporal whispered.

"I'd like you to give me back-up. Do you think you could make it up to that window ledge, if someone gave you a shove-up?"

"Of course, I could, sir," Matz answered loyally. "Inspite of the pegleg," he tapped his wooden leg, "I'll be up there like a frigging chimp."

Von Dodenburg smiled at him. "Good man," he hissed. "Come on, let's go." He nodded to the men with the bags of grenades. They knew what he wanted, without orders. Two of them bent, clapped their hands together tightly and prepared to take the strain.

In one and the same movement, von Dodenburg balanced himself on their hands and heaved himself upwards to the window ledge. He flashed a glance inside. There was no one close to it. He nodded. Lightly as a cat, he dropped to the dirty, unswept floor and crouched there as Matz followed him.

The nave was crowded with drunken, sweating soldiers, all dressed in German uniforms, devoid of all badges of rank and German insignia. Most of them were gnawing at chunks of meat, the grease running down their unshaven chins, while the cooks toiled with yet another looted pig at the spit above the great crackling fire. Matz sniffed and whispered, "Deserters seem to get better fodder."

Von Dodenburg nodded, but didn't take his gaze off the scene: the desecrated church, the drunken brutalized wretches who had once been decent German infantrymen, the complete breakdown of military discipline. Somehow it symbolised, at that moment, everything which had happened at Stalingrad, including their own cowardly withdrawal. He grimaced, actual pain mirrored in his lean handsome face, as if someone had just slid a sharp knife into his ribs.

Then he saw him. There was no mistaking that hard scarred face, the result of two years of sabre-duelling in one of the pre-war university *Burschenshaften*.* "Hanno," he gasped with absolute, total shock. Hanno von Einem."

---

* German university duelling clubs, forbidden by Hitler. But they continued to function all the same.

Chapter Four

The von Einems had been like the von Dodenburgs. Both were impoverished East Prussians, rich in land, but poor in money, who lived on an annual meagre potato crop and whatever pensions, military or otherwise, which the family heads had obtained after years of service to the state.

As boys they had gone to the same village school together, long-legged, barefoot children with flaxen hair, who were bored with Fraulein Noske and her attempts to teach them *'schoenschreiben'*, correct copper-plate handwriting, longing for the moment when she sounded the bell and they could escape to the village pond to swim naked with the other boys or go fishing with rods from bamboo canes, with a hooked pin attached to the line.

They had been the best of friends. Kuno von Dodenburg had been "Mr Dead Mountain", a pun on his name; while Hanno had been "Mr One", a pun on his name as well. In those hot East Prussian summers when each day seemed to last an eternity, they had spent hours playing and talking of what they would become once they were grown up, a stage of their life which couldn't come soon enough for both of them, "I shall become a general like my father," Kuno would declare, to which Hanno would invariably reply, "Not me. My father was a general too, but it cost him one eye and one leg. I shall be rich and famous and retain my bits and pieces."

"Boo to you, capitalist!" von Dodenburg often would taunt his friend, hardly knowing what a capitalist was, for there were none on the impoverished Junkers estates of his native East Prussia; then Hanno would launch himself at the much taller von Dodenburg and they would waltz around in the dusty path, punching each other in a half-hearted manner.

In the mid-thirties, Hanno had gone to Breslau University to study law and had immediately joined one of the 'fighting associations'. "I know, I know, Kuno," he had protested when his friend had reminded him of his childhood statement that he wasn't going to 'lose his bits and pieces', "we do chop bits of each other's faces off, But we do make important connections, useful in later life. All those former members, now important people, love nothing better than to come to Breslau and have a good piss-up with us young foxes."

As soon as war had broken out, as an officer of the reserve, Hanno von Einem had been called up for active service immediately. Through the army grapevine, Kuno von Dodenburg had heard of his exploits in Poland and later in France. One year later in 1941, Hanno had been the first of his year to win the coveted Knight's Cross of the Iron Cross for his exploits in holding off a whole Russian battalion with a handful of German infantrymen, each one of them wounded including himself. It had been headline news at the time and in the German Newsreel Hanno von Einem had been photographed accepting the decoration from no less a person than a beaming Führer himself.

Now, von Dodenburg wondered as he crouched there in the gloom, staring as if mesmerized at his old school friend. What had happened to him, scion of a line of

Prussian Junkers who had served their monarch loyally for three hundred years? How had he come to be associated with this drunken mutinous rabble?

"Sir." Matz nudged him discreetly. It jerked von Dodenburg out of his reverie.

Carefully von Dodenburg rose to his feet, pulling out his pistol, while Matz covered him with his schmeisser, tucked tightly into his right hip. "On a count of three," he whispered to the little corporal and clicked off his safety catch.

Three! Without hesitation von Dodenburg pulled the trigger. Once . . . twice . . . three times. Plaster rained down from the once ornate roof. The tight confines of the nave echoed and re-echoed with the noise of the three slugs.

Men dropped bottles. Others stared, meat dangling stupidly from their greasy mouths. A few looked as if they might reach for their weapons, but Matz's threatening jerk with his machine pistol told them it would be safer not to do so.

"All right," von Dodenburg said in a calm, cool voice, "Everyone put up their hands. Nice and gently. Then there'll be no trouble. *Wirds bald?*" he snapped suddenly, iron in his voice now.

As one their hands shot up, save one pair, those of Hanno von Einem. The latter said, a half smile on his face, his voice as cool as von Dodenburg's, "I don't suppose you'd shoot me, Kuno, what?"

Von Dodenburg looked at him coldly, though his mind was racing, "If I have to, I shall," he said and motioned with his pistol.

Hanno gave a little shrug and raising his hands, looked at his old schoolmate with a look that was almost akin to contempt.

Still holding his pistol levelled at the mutineers, faces crimson and sullen in the ruddy light cast by the fire, above which the second pig steamed and spat, untended, slowly going black, von Dodenburg reach for his whistle. He shrilled a blast on it. It was the signal. Suddenly the young grenadiers exploded into the nave, weapons at the ready, to stop suddenly and stare at the strange scene.

"All right, Matz," von Dodenburg commanded, "take care of 'em. I want a word with that officer." Purposefully, though he had never felt less purposeful, he elbowed his way through the sullen mob to where von Einem stood, a kind of mocking smile on his scarred face.

"Hanno, what – how did you get into this mess?"

"May I put my hands down? Bit of a strain, you know."

"Of course." Von Dodenburg thrust his pistol into its holster as a sign that he intended to discuss whatever had to be discussed on the basis of their old friendship with one another.

"Thanks." Hanno von Einem lowered his hands gratefully. "Well, how are you?" he asked, as if there was nothing unusual about the way they had met again after all these years.

"Cut out the bullshit, Hanno!" von Dodenburg snapped, suddenly a little angry. "What have you got to do with this mob?"

"This *mob*," he emphasized the word, "is all that remains of the two companies I once commanded. Two hundred men out of four hundred and fifty. Fifty-five percentage casualties in a week."

"Well, we've all suffered casualties in the past, as you well know, but we've never mutinied."

Hanno drew a deep breath like a man who was preparing to dive from the high board. "Listen, Kuno,"

97

he commenced slowly. "It is not a question of mutiny any more."

"What is it then?" von Dodenburg demanded.

"*Revolution!*"

"What did you say?"

"I'm sure you heard me quite well, Kuno," Hanno said. "Where have your eyes been ever since you came to Russia first? You know we came to this country, promising the people to free them from a Soviet dictatorship. What happened in fact?" He thrust forward his face, suddenly angry and flushed, "I shall tell you, if you don't already know. We have imposed on this vast country a tyranny far worse than anything Stalin, the Soviet dictator, could ever have done. You've seen the Russian POW camps, filled with half-starved wretches, all skin and bone, eating from troughs like animals. You've seen what they – no, *we* – have done to the Soviet Jews—"

"Stop this madness," von Dodenburg barked harshly, finger twitching on the trigger of his pistol. "Where is this conversation going? What are you trying to say, man?"

"This: Hitler and his foul mob must go," Hanno declared, eyes blazing. "They are worse than the communists can ever be. I, for one, will work with them, to ensure that the Hitler pack vanishes from the face of this earth as soon as possible."

"*What*, a pact with the Devil?" von Dodenburg snorted, feeling his anger grow by the instant. "What do you think that Russian swine would do to our homeland, once he had conquered it—"

Hanno opened his mouth to answer, but he was beaten to it by a very calm voice, speaking excellent, though slightly accented, German which said, "We are not cannibals or barbarians, you know. I don't think we have eaten anyone for breakfast for quite a while now."

Von Dodenburg turned startled. A woman was standing there, clad in a shining black leather coat, which failed to conceal an excellent figure, riding breeches and highly polished boots. But it was the face that caught von Dodenburg's attention. Most Russian women he had met behind the front had had heavy-set peasant faces with large bulbous noses.

This woman's face was admittedly slavic, with the Slav's slanting cheekbones and eyes. But otherwise, it was beautiful, with green eyes set against a perfect skin, exuding a strange sensual charm which almost made von Dodenburg forget his present danger. "Who . . . who are you?" he stuttered, as the woman nodded to von Einem as if in approval. Obviously they had met before.

"Colonel Elena Kirova of the Women's Death Head Regiment," the woman clicked her heels together in almost the Prussian fashion and touched her gloved hand to her cap in salute. "And you are the redoubtable Major von Dodenburg of SS Assault Regiment Wotan."

Von Einem grinned at the look of utter surprise on his old school-friend's face, as the latter stuttered, "How . . . how do you know this?"

She shrugged and her breasts moved delightfully under the tight black leather of her uniform coat. "Easy. My regiment has just – er – taken over your people outside. They talked."

"Well, I'll shit a brick!" Matz exclaimed, as now more and more of the black uniformed women started to enter the nave, all of them heavily armed and formidable. Slowly, reluctantly, he started to lower his machine pistol and then as one of the Russian amazons, her belt heavy with stick grenades, jerked her tommy gun threateningly in his direction, he dropped it to the floor.

For a moment – later it seemed to a bemused von

Dodenburg to be an eternity – the church was frozen into a tableau of surprise, bewilderment and uncertainty, as von Dodenburg, brain racing electrically, tried to assess this completely new situation.

Colonel Kirova did it for him. "Let me explain, Major," she said in that delightfully accented German of hers. "I and Major von Einem have already talked."

So that was it, the thought flashed through von Dodenburg's mind. Hanno von Einem had not just deserted; he had also made contact with the enemy. Obviously the ex-lawyer was playing it safe.

"At this present moment," the Russian woman continued, "the Red Army is preparing to make a full-scale assault on the Karpovka River area, some ten kilometres from here, heading for the gap conveniently made for us by *Comrade*," she emphasized the word, as if it were of some significance, "von Einem's defection. Now all that stands in the path of our complete breakthrough and attack into the Sixth Army's flank is your own armoured regiment – Wotan."

"So?" von Dodenburg heard himself saying, as if from a very long way off, as he tried to absorb all this new and startling information.

"So, my dear Major," the Russian woman said, staring at him in a bold, almost provocative manner, which despite the tension, made him feel the first faint stirrings of his loins, "Wotan has already deserted the front." She held up her gloved hand, as if she expected him to protest at the information. "Yes, we know that. In a manner, you have voted with your feet."

"How do you mean?"

"You have left your positions because you knew they were untenable – that the Sixth Army is doomed. Indeed the whole of the German Army is doomed." She said the words with an air of finality, as if there could be no doubt about the truth of her statement.

"Don't you see, Kuno," Hanno von Einem broke in eagerly, "this is *your* – and *my* – chance to help create a new Germany. There are already several of us in the Sixth, including general officers, who are prepared to assist our new Russian comrades in the great task of bringing about the downfall of that tyrannt Hitler so that we can replace him and his regime with a better Germany."

"*Assist*?" von Dodenburg seized on the word, as his head whirled and whirled. "How do you mean?"

Colonel Kirova answered for Hanno. "*Fight*!" she said. "Fight at our side. Then you will have earned the right to decide on Germany's future."

Kuno von Dodenburg stared at her and then at Hanno, as if he suspected that they were both mad. Finally, he managed to stutter, "Did you . . . say . . . fight? . . . Fight against my own countrymen?"

"Yes," the Russian woman snapped. "You shall see, Major von Dodenburg. Before this year of 1942 is out, the Free German Army will be fighting at the side of our Red Army against the Hitlerian beast. Comrade Stalin has already decreed it. So it will happen. You, Major von Dodenburg, can be a member of that great force if you help us now—"

"*Stop*!" von Dodenburg bellowed, slapping his hands to his ears to cut out their voices. "*Stop, I'll hear no more of this treason*!"

Colonel Kirova shrugged, her beautiful face showing no emotion. "Then," she said very simply, "you must die . . ."

Chapter Five

Himmler was almost pathetically grateful. Boldt could almost feel his gratitude over the one thousand kilometre distance which separated them, as he told the *Reichsfuhrer* what he had seen on the Karpovka River. Over and over again, Himmler kept saying, "Thank God for my SS . . . They're the fire brigade of the Eastern Front . . . always there to put out the blaze when it is at its fiercest . . ."

"I have other news for you, *Reichsfuhrer*," Boldt said when finally the *Reichsfuhrer* stopped babbling, admitting something which he had known all along but dared not speak of even to the other members of his squadron.

"Yes, go on, Boldt," Himmler said eagerly.

"I'm pretty certain that SS Assault Regiment Wotan is roughly in the same area where the Ivans intend to cross the river. I spotted one of their Tigers which had been knocked out by the enemy," he confessed at last.

"Well, this indeed is excellent news. First you tell me that my own SS Black Hawks have spotted the Russian attack. Now this. I cannot tell you just how happy you make me, Boldt, *very happy!*" Himmler quavered.

"Shit on shingle," Boldt told himself, as he listened to that reedy, excited voice, "he's going to shoot his wad into his pants in a minute."

"I shall inform the Führer at once," Himmler went on excitedly. "As usual my SS took the initiative without higher authority, especially when it comes from the *Wehrmacht*. Colonel Geier didn't defect with his regiment. He simply rode to the sound of the guns. Yes, the Führer must know this immediately, Boldt."

"*Jawohl, Reichsfuhrer,*" Boldt said dutifully. Outside on the field, the ground crews had finished sweeping away the new snow on the runway. Now they were searing the frostbound concrete with what looked like giant blow torches, while machanics ran back and forth preparing the Stukas for take-off.

"One thing, Boldt, before I approach the Führer," Himmler said, "Have you been able yet to make contact with Wotan?"

"Not yet, *Reichsfuhrer*" Boldt said. "But the fog has lifted and it has stopped snowing at long last. On the approach flight to bomb the Russian bridgehead, if they have succeeded already in getting across, I shall attempt to make visual contact with Wotan. Perhaps Colonel Geier will be able to radio signal his intentions to von Manstein's command and they, in their turn, will be able to contact you and relay them to SS HQ."

"Excellent . . . excellent," Himmler chortled and Boldt could visualize him rubbing his skinny hands together, as if they were dirty and needed washing which he always did when he was excited as he was now. "Believe you me, there's a promotion in this for you, my dear fellow."

"Thank you, sir."

"Now, I must not delay you any longer. Speed is of the essence. But keep me posted immediately there are any new developments. Good luck to you and your brave chaps. *Ende.*"

Bertha looked up from her typewriter and said gushingly, "How well you handled that, Heini. You didn't reveal one bit how worried you really were about this Wotan business."

He put on his 'war face' which he practised every morning in front of his shaving mirror (though he really didn't need to shave every morning) and said, "When you're at the top, little darling, you must never show your emotions. That can be thought of as weakness, and a commander who has to send in men to battle, perhaps to die, must never show weakness."

She pouted a little. "But you will show a little weakness with me now and again, my dear cheetah, won't you?" she simpered and reached over for the front of his breeches.

He drew back as if stung. "There is no time for that sort of thing *now*, Bertha," he said firmly. "There are great affairs of state in progress. I must not dissipate my strength."

"Of course, of course," she agreed readily and bending her head over the typewriter, she started to type his latest letter to an SS man, who had written to protest that he had been at the front in Russia ever since 1941 and his wife had already produced two babies with other men, "The *Reichsfuhrer* details me to inform you that your wife is carrying out important war work and must not be regarded as a rotten little whore who needs to keep her pants in the ice-box because they are so 'hot' (as you phrase it). The Folk needs children to make up for the losses at the front. She obviously is doing her best to ensure that those losses are made up. Therefore I say to you . . ."

Boldt strode into the ready-room, where his pilots, already dressed in their flying gear, were stowing away their lucky mascots – teddy bears, rabbit feet, women's frilly knickers and all the rest of the rubbish without which they wouldn't fly, and snapped. "All right, silence in the whorehouse. Hands off yer cocks and on with yer socks."

There were the usual hoots and someone rang the bell, hanging over the makeshift bar, which was always rung when they commenced celebrating a victory. Baron Karst slapped his riding crop against his highly polished boot and exclaimed, "A-hunting we will go no doubt, what?"

"Exactly," Boldt snapped. These are my orders, confirmed by the *Reichsfuhrer*."

"Good for the *Reichsfuhrer*," someone chortled. "Oh, how we love the dear old *Reichsfuhrer!*"

"Oh, shut up, you undisciplined bunch of shits," Boldt cried above the racket. "Let's get on. All right, we've got to knock out the Ivan bridgehead – usual dive-bombing stuff," he added almost casually, knowing that his blue-blooded, irreverent pilots would not stand for a lecture on the tactics of such an operation. "At the same time we've got to find Wotan and try to put the ground jobs in the big picture."

"What about that three day pass to gay Parree?" someone asked.

Boldt ignored the remark and went on to say, "I have a rough idea where Wotan will be. I'm hoping, therefore, once we've finished our attack, Colonel Geier and his armour will be able to drive straight at the Ivans, while they're still disorganized, and see them off rather sharpish. Questions?" he asked, as always at the end of a briefing, though he knew they never had any questions. It would have meant losing face by appearing not to know everything. They all think of themselves as frigging Jesus walking across the water, he had remarked bitterly to himself about them more than once. Now, suddenly, he realized he didn't like these affected aristos on the make. "All right," he snapped, "that's it. Let's get on the stick."

There was a scrape of chairs and a shuffle of feet. The pilots rose lazily and wandered off towards the doorway, folding their maps, fiddling with their equipment, leaving Boldt to stare at their backs and wonder again at their casual flippancy in the face of imminent death. It was something, he decided, he would never understand. Perhaps it came with the blue blood that flowed through their veins. He dismissed the matter and followed them out into the freezing cold.

The tension was palpable, as the ground crews readied the squadron for take-off. Mechanics lay full length on the freezing runway, holding the chocs, as the pilots started to gun their engines prior to take-off. Senior NCOs ran from aircraft to aircraft ticking off their check-lists. Over at the little wooden control tower, standing beneath the wind sock, the ground commander poised with his flare pistol. He would fire a green flare to signal take-off. Round the field, off-duty ground personnel, huddled in every bit of clothing, stamped their feet and waited to wave the pilots off as was the squadron's tradition. They'd be out there again, Boldt knew, anxiously surveying the sky for any losses.

The senior crew chief, a grizzled portly staff sergeant, who rumour had it had once served under the great Red Baron himself in the old war, threw Boldt a tremendous salute. "Weather's just told me, sir, no snow for the next four hours." His habitual broad smile vanished from his fat red face. "Please keep your eyes skinned, sir," he warned. "Yer never know with—"

He didn't finish his sentence, but Boldt knew what he meant. "Don't worry, Heinz old house. The glassy orbs will be kept as skinned as tinned tomatoes," Boldt said. "All right, give me a leg-up."

The old NCO cradled his horny palms and heaved Boldt into the cockpit. Boldt nodded to the observer who did the same in reply. Then he gunned the engine. The Stuka trembled at every rivet, as if it might disintegrate at any moment. Satisfied that the engine was running true and sweet, Boldt slackened his pressure on the throttle and turned his attention on the still figure standing on the observation platform of the control tower. The ground controller had already raised his pistol. In a few seconds they'd be airborne.

Suddenly – startlingly – the stubby Yak fighter, bearing the red star of the Soviet Air Force, flashed across the field, machine guns blazing. The ground controller clutched his chest, as behind him the windows of the control tower shattered, and fell to his knees. As the Yak soared into the sky, tiny deadly black eggs dropped from its belly. Behind it, the flak opened up, tracer surging upwards and then falling short, as the Russian squeezed every bit of power out of his plane. The bombs straddled the field. A Stuka fell to one side as its under-carriage gave way like a bird that had abruptly injured one leg. Boldt felt the blast slam into his own plane. It rocked wildly and for one crazy moment, Boldt thought his Stuka might be blown over. It steadied and he flung a wild glance out of the cockpit. Poor Heinz lay there minus his head, which was rolling away down the tarmac like a ball abandoned by a careless child. But Boldt had no time for the dead NCO now. It was vital to get airborne at once. That Yak would be reporting to its own field at this very moment. The Soviets would know they were coming. He opened the throttle and surged forward. The others followed, dodging the steaming brown bombholes. Behind them,

Baron Karst died screaming and trapped in the cockpit of the wrecked Stuka. As he rolled by him, Boldt said, almost unconsciously and without pity, "Well your frigging crop and riding boots didn't help you this time, did they?" A moment later, he was airborne.

Chapter Six

"I was once in a boozer – Berlin, I think," Matz was saying, "when a drunk walked in and said to the barmaid, 'I fucked you last year around Christmas time. Don't you remember?'"

The Wotan troopers squatted in the freezing crypt, their breath fogging the icy air as they listened to Matz in gloomy silence. Upstairs in the nave, the drinking had ceased now that the Russian woman had appeared so mysteriously, and they could hear the steady tread of sentries, as if Hannon von Einem had managed to restore some kind of order in his drunken mob of mutineers.

"The barmaid said, *'Verpisse dich'** – in a nice sort of way," Matz continued in his attempts to cheer up his fellow captives, who all knew they wouldn't survive this day if von Dodenburg didn't agree to the Russian terms. "Nothing nasty – nothing like that. But the drunk wouldn't have it. He said, 'So yer don't remember me mug. But I bet you'll remember this.' And do you know what?" Matz looked around the circle of faces with a fake smile on his own. "He pulls his old bazooka out of his britches and plonks it down on the counter. But that's not the end of it. The barmaid looks at his tool and then as cool as cucumber, she takes

---

* Roughly "Piss off". *Transl.*

the fork that they use to get the pickled eggs out of the jar, and she pins his cock down with it to the bar. Did that drunk howl? By the Great Whore of Buxtehude where the dogs bark with their tails, he let out a roar that you could have heard at the other side of the world!"

Matz beamed at them, noting as he did so that his tale of ancient lecheries was having little effect on his comrades. They looked as miserable as ever.

Von Dodenburg nodded his approval, as Matz lapsed into silence. He was typical 'old hare'. He appeared to let nothing ever get him down and always did his best to cheer up the 'greenbeaks', as they called the young recruits. Wrily he told himself, he, himself, needed some cheering up. For the situation in which he found himself was really grim. Never would he consider allying himself with the Soviets and fighting against his own people. He felt physically sick at the very thought. Yet if he didn't, not only he but also his men, would die. He was quite sure that the beautiful Russian colonel was as hard as nails. As for Hanno von Einem, he wouldn't attempt to stop her and her "Death Battalions". Hanno, he realised, had become a typical German opportunist, one of those Germans he had always hated who would change their beliefs as often as he would change his shirt. Cost what it may, Hanno von Einem wanted to be on the side of the winners, and he had decided that they were going to be the Russians.

"Now you young punks," Matz was saying, "think you invented sex – think you know all about it. Well, I'll tell yer something – for nothing." He leaned forward and stared aggressively around the circle of pale, miserable faces. "How many of you wet dreams could satisfy a piece of gash – *who had been living with an ape for six months?* Now tell me that, eh? 'Cos it takes some dong to compete with a fully grown banana-scoffer, you'd better believe me."

Von Dodenburg let Matz's words drone into the far distance as he forced himself to try to think the situation through. The village was firmly in the hands of the Russian women soldiers and their new German allies. Yet the bulk of Wotan's armour, under the command of the Vulture, was still at liberty. With the score or so Tiger tanks he had available, the Vulture was more than a match for a whole Soviet infantry division. The Russians had no tank which could tackle that sixty-ton monster. Von Dodenburg's brow wrinkled with frustration. The question was – how was he to contact the Vulture and those metal monsters of his? "Yes," a harsh, cynical little voice at the back of his mind added, "and even if you could, would the Vulture risk the success of his 'withdrawal' in order to tackle the Ivans?"

He dabbed his brow with his handkerchief, for despite the freezing cold of the crypt, he felt warm, even hot. He guessed it had something to do with nervous tension. What in three devils' name was he going to do?

"I mean, she wasn't exactly my collar size," Matz was saying. He looked at his broken, filthy nails as if in mock modesty. "Not that I'm saying I'm not well hung. I mean, you've just got to look at my rounded shoulders to see I'm carrying considerable weight down there between my legs . . ."

Wearily von Dodenburg wished the wizened little corporal would shut up. He couldn't seem to think with Matz going on about his sexual adventures, real or imagined. But he knew it was nothing to do with Matz. It was the problem of making that overwhelming decision, which would determine the fate of those honest German boys who were listening to his tall tales. It was a matter of conscience – *his* conscience.

"*Sir*", a familiar voice broke suddenly into his reverie. His heart leapt. "Sir," the voice said again urgently, "it's me . . . Up here, sir."

Von Dodenburg flung up his head. In the middle of the circle, Matz breathed, "As I frigging live and breathe – holy strawsack, it's frigging Schulzi."

"Who the frigging hell did you frigging think it was – a dick-docking frigging rabbi from Rumania," Schulze exclaimed, as he lowered himself carefully from the conduit which apparently ran the length of the crypt's ceiling, breathing hard and knocking off the dust of centuries as he did so.

"Where did—" Matz began.

But a triumphant Schulze beat his old comrade to it. "The frigging Popovs locked me up. But you can't keep a Schulze long behind lock and key. We've had centuries of experience in our family of getting out from behind Swedish curtains." He spread the fingers of his right hand over his broad grinning face to indicate he meant prison bars. "As soon as I found the key, I was out in zero-comma-nothing."

Looking at Schulze's happy, cheeky face, von Dodenburg felt a faint surge of renewed hope. Perhaps there was a way out for them as well. "What's it look like up there?" he asked.

"The place is lousy with Popov gash. God only knows why women want to play soldier boy when they're a lot more useful on their backs with their legs spread, I'll never know." He saw the look in von

Dodenburg's eyes and continued hurriedly. "I reckon there must be a whole battalion of them in and around the church. They've sharpened up that lot of deadbeat stubble-hoppers as well. They're standing to arms and there's no more fire-water being tilted down their greedy sodding throats either." Schulze licked his cracked lips, as if he would not have minded indulging in a little "fire-water" at that particular moment himself.

Von Dodenburg considered a few moments before addressing the men. "As I see it, comrades," he said softly. "Colonel Geier will have passed this village by now, thinking his flank is safe. We haven't reported anything because obviously we can't, so he will have pushed on with armour. So that will make him vulnerable to attack from both sides, once the Ivans have crossed the river and that – er – rather attractive lady colonel up there learns we are not going to help her."

The men looked grim. They realised von Dodenburg had made his decision not to cooperate and that meant their lives were forfeit if he could find no way out of the mess they were currently in.

Von Dodenburg realised what they were thinking and he hastily said, "Comrades, you know Wotan's old motto – march or croak. Well, we're not going to croak, I can assure you of that. We've got to get out of this place before the balloon goes up!" He looked pointedly at Schulze.

The big NCO rose to the bait immediately. "Well, sir," he said, "what goes in has to come out, as the pavement pounder said to the punter with the limp dong." If he had expected a laugh at what he thought was a very witty sally, he was disappointed. The Wotan troopers were much too eager to hear whether he had some means of getting them out of the trap in which they found themselves.

"Get on with it," von Dodenburg urged.

"It's still light outside and we take a chance that the Popovs might spot us once we get out of the church. But at least I can get you out of the church."

"Good man," von Dodenburg snapped. "All right, comrades, boots off first and tie your footrags around them so that you'll not make any noise*."

"Yes," Schulze growled, clenching a fist like a small steam shovel, "anyone making a noise will have me to deal with."

"Oh," one Flipper simpered in what he thought was a female voice, "say no more, Sergeant Schulze. You're frightening me. I think I'm going to have my monthlies."

But swiftly the men did as they were commanded. Schulze waited impatiently till they were finished, then he ordered, "All right, we'll spread out . . . after me." Effortlessly, he reached up and placed his lower body nearly into the ancient tunnel. He squirmed round so that his upper body was hanging downwards and said, "All right, you first Matz."

Matz grasped his comrade's hands and was drawn up without even a gasp on Schulze's part. Schulze disappeared. Then it was Matz's turn to haul up the next man. One by one they started to disappear into the narrow tunnel, watched by von Dodenburg, his heart beating urgently, for he knew it took only one glance through the barred door of the crypt for a sentry to shout the alarm. Then it was his turn. Hastily he grabbed the

---

* In the German Army, instead of socks, the soldiers wrapped cloths around their feet.

trooper's arm and felt himself being raised. Neatly and deftly he turned, and entered the tunnel. A moment later he was crawling after the others down the length of the dim, stinking tunnel which he hoped and prayed fervently led to freedom.

Chapter Seven

The Vulture was worried. It was getting dark and black shadows were racing across the lonely snowbound steppe. It was four hours since he had last heard from von Dodenburg and the Vulture knew once darkness fell, his Tigers would be very vulnerable to lone Ivans stalking them with rocket-launchers. He needed the protection against them which von Dodenburg's panzer grenadiers would have provided.

"Damn von Dodenburg," he snapped to Creeping Jesus above the roar of the Tiger's mighty engines, "where in three devils' name is the man? Why hasn't he reported in?"

Creeping Jesus could hardly conceal his delight. "Well, you know what Major von Dodenburg is like, sir?" he said, savouring the knowledge that that arrogant swine von Dodenburg was in for a rocket when he did finally turn up. "He always seems to think he knows best and tosses the book out of the window." He smirked at the Vulture.

The Vulture didn't respond. His mind was too full of the problem on hand. For the last two hours there had been persistent gunfire from the direction of the river, accompanied by heavy Russian rocket barrages, but there had been no German response. "It's almost as if the front has gone to bed for the night," he had snorted angrily to Creeping Jesus next to him in the turret of the lead Tiger. "It's pretty obvious that the Popovs are preparing for a crossing of the Karpovka, but our people seem to be doing nothing."

Now as the darkening sky began to be lit by the fiery scarlet of the Soviet barrage, increasing in fury by the minute, he knew that it wouldn't be long before the Soviets started their crossing. And a Soviet attack was something he, personally, didn't want to be involved in. Yet at the same time, could he risk continuing to move after dark? "Dammit," he snapped angrily out loud, "we're caught between the devil and the deep blue sea. If we keep on moving, some ragged-arsed Popov partisan might shove a rocket up our arses. If we stop, we might just get a basinful of what is beginning to start over there." He nodded in the direction of the river.

Creeping Jesus shivered, as he realised the danger they were in. "Perhaps von Dodenburg and his grenadiers will turn up before darkness, sir," he said, his voice already beginning to quaver.

Again the Vulture didn't respond to his adjutant's words. Instead he prepared to make his decision. It was just then that the flak lookout manning the four 20mm anti-aircraft guns of the flak wagon in the centre of the long convoy of half-tracks crawling over that endless plain yelled, "Aircraft . . . three o'clock!" Next moment he swung his cannon round to meet any possible danger from that quarter, while the loaders tensed with packs of 20mm shells in their arms.

The Vulture thrust up his glasses and peered to his right. Black sinister shapes slid into the gleaming, calibrated circles of glass. Next to him a worried Creeping Jesus did the same.

The Vulture identified the approaching planes almost

immediately. There was no mistaking that gull-like wing shape. "Junkers 87," he announced, "Stuka dive bombers!"

Creeping Jesus breathed a sigh of relief and said, "Thank God for that."

The Vulture kept his binoculars firmly fixed on the Stukas. "We're not out of the shit yet, Adjutant," he rasped harshly. "They might be looking for us, *remember*."

Creeping Jesus's face fell.

Now the squadron of planes came lower and lower, slowing down to almost stalling speed. The watchers could see the black crosses painted on their fuselage quite clearly. Creeping Jesus tugged at the strap of his helmet, as if preparing himself for the bombs soon to come.

The Vulture lowered his glasses. "They're the Black Hawk Squadron, the SS's own flight," he rasped, telling himself that it would be typical of that bespectacled, knock kneed idiot Himmler to send out his own planes to deal with Wotan. "Here they come!" he cried, as the lead plane peeled off and started to drop out of the darkening sky.

"Oh my God!" Creeping Jesus exclaimed fearfully. "They're not going to bomb us, are they?"

"We'll soon find out," the Vulture said grimly.

"But—" the rest of Creeping Jesus's words were drowned by the roar of the Stuka's engines, as it swept along the length of the column, dragging its evil black shadow behind it. Then the Stuka was soaring high back to join the rest of the Black Hawks, leaving behind it a small parachute slowly drifting down to the steppe. Moments later, the Black Hawks were roaring away at full speed to the river.

Screwing his monocle more firmly into his right eye,

the Vulture read the message which had been carried down by the little chute, while a breathless Creeping Jesus, who had fetched it, listened impatiently. *"Enemy attempting to form bridgehead over R. Karpovka . . . south of Rogachik . . . Reichsführer SS orders SS Wotan to counter-attack immediately in that direction . . . River must be held at all costs . . . Boldt, Squadron Leader."*

Wordlessly the Vulture handed it to Creeping Jesus and stared to the south, mind racing, as he considered Himmler's order. Wotan had been located now and he knew that if he didn't obey the *Reichsführer's* command, the latter would take action against him. But the Pocket was already doomed and although his Tigers would undoubtedly hold up the Popovs for a little while, in the end, Wotan would be wiped out – for nothing.

"What are we going to do, sir?" Creeping Jesus asked, as he stowed the message away in his book.

"Well, we are not going to attack – that's for certain."

"But if we disobey the *Reichsführer's* order, we will be severely punished."

"I know that." Suddenly the Vulture grinned. It wasn't a pleasant sight. "So let him believe that we are attacking and then undoubtedly the fortunes of war will turn against us, and we shall have to break off that attack. Now this is what we're going to do . . ."

The area of the river was spread out beneath the eight planes like a map: the dark green mass of the fir forests, the infinite white range of the steppe, tiny straw-roof huts clustered in hamlets hanging onto the banks of the Karpovka as if glued there.

Boldt took it all in in a few seconds, especially the hundreds of tiny black figures scurrying around on the left bank of the river next to the pre-fabricated bridge which already had almost met up with the opposite bank.

In his position in front of the tight squadron box, as the Stukas seemed to hover above the silver snake of the river, like great black metal birds-of-prey, Boldt felt himself overcome by the old sense of elation. At that moment, he was all-powerful, capable of dealing death and destruction on all he surveyed.

Suddenly all doubts vanished. He felt on top of his form. His eyes were bright and keen. His every muscle tense, firm and ready. Behind him, knowing what was going to happen in a couple of seconds, the observer tightened his straps, swung the machine gun round in a circle, noting that it moved with well-greased, easy precision.

"*Tallyho!*" Boldt yelled. He jerked the stick forward. The Stuka's nose tilted frantically. Next moment the dive-bomber was falling out the sky, plunging towards the ground at a tremendous rate.

The Russian flak opened up at once. Golden balls of fire curved up to meet Boldt, increasing their speed by the second. In a flash, the sky was peppered with black puffs of angry smoke. Tracer zipped back and forth in a lethal morse. Now the whole landscape below was wreathed in flame and smoke, Boldt sailed on and on. He was carried away by a wild ecstasy that was almost sexual. He altered his angle of dive from sixty degrees to seventy and then to eighty, his sirens shrieking like banshees.

The bridge loomed up larger and larger. He could see the Russian engineers running wildly to get away from it. Some simply dropped their tools and dived over the side. A few picked up rifles and started blazing away at the diving plane purposelessly.

Boldt hit the brake rudder. The flaps below the wings came down. The Stuka staggered in mid-air. Boldt felt the flesh of his face slammed against the bones. For one brief moment he blacked out. He came to just in time to see the Yak fighter hurtling towards him. He pressed the tit. The bombs fell from his wings. In that same instant he caught a glimpse of more Russian Yak fighters hurrying towards him, guns blazing.

Boldt broke to the left. Tracer streamed by him. To the rear the observer started pounding the sky with his machine gun. All was noise, smoke, confusion and sudden death. Boldt flashed a glance below. Great whirling white fountains were erupting down there. But the damned bridge had not been hit. Nor was it likely to be now. He could see that, for there seemed to be Yaks everywhere, diving and twisting, breaking up the Black Hawks' formation.

Boldt pressed his throat mike. "*Jettison . . . jettison!*" he yelled urgently, knowing the slow, obsolete Stukas, especially with a full load of bombs aboard, were no match for the Russian fighters. "Do a bunk—" He broke off, as he spotted, among the dark hurrying shapes of the jettisoned bombs, the Yak pouring lead into one of his planes. Its wing tore off and came fluttering down in circles like a metal leaf. Next moment it fell out of the sky, screeching to its death.

Boldt had seen enough. The sweat standing out in great opaque pearls on his forehead, he brought the Stuka almost to ground level, putting off the Yak pilot who had attached himself to the plane's tail – at least momentarily. Then he was roaring down the banks of the great river, bullets rapping the Stuka's fuselage like the beak of a giant woodpecker. But Boldt was not worried by the small arms fire. He concentrated in avoiding the obstacles on both sides. One false move now and they'd be finished. He flashed over the nearly finished bridge. It was littered with dead bodies, but it was totally undamaged. Then he swung round a bend in the river gorge, leaving the noise and smoke of the battle behind. He had done it again, escaped with a whole skin, though God only knew what had happened to the Black Hawks.

They'd done their bit. But the bridge over the Karpovka was still intact. Now it was up the Vulture and his Tigers.

Chapter Eight

"*Driver – driver advance!*" von Dodenburg yelled, as all down the line of halftracks, the engines burst into furious life. Suddenly the cold night air was filled with the cloying stench of petrol. With a rusty creak, the vehicles, packed with the young panzer grenadiers, started to move off, while von Dodenburg in the lead halftrack stared impatiently to his front.

They had moved noiselessly through the Russian lines as they had done often enough before when they had been trapped behind the enemy; and within ten minutes they had been safely outside the village heading for where the halftracks were parked. Von Dodenburg had wasted no time. He had ordered the escapers to be re-armed with what extra weapons there were in the vehicles. Now he wanted to take his revenge on Hanno von Einem for his treachery, and, though he wouldn't have admitted it to anyone, to confront that beautiful, if supercilious Russian lady colonel one more time.

The lead halftrack breasted the hill and burst through the firs lining its downward slope, scattering leaves and branches in a green rain. Down in the village, there were sudden shouts of alarm. Someone shrilled a whistle urgently. Lights flicked on. A red flare sailed into the star-studded velvet sky, exploded and bathed everything below in a glowing unreal scarlet.

"*Blast 'em!*" von Dodenburg yelled above the racket, as he himself fired a star shell from the tubes attached to the side of the halftrack.

The star shell exploded in a glare of blinding white light to their front, in the same instant that the halftrack's gunner opened up with his spandau, spinning the weapon from side to side and hosing the *isbas* with a thousand rounds per minute. It was standard Wotan operating procedure. Keep the enemy's heads down with this wild indiscriminate firing, while at the same time blinding any Popov gunner with the star shell flare.

They barrelled through the trees. Without any command needed to be given out, the halftrack drivers extended to left and right to present a smaller target. Now they rattled and raced towards the Russian village in a great armoured "V", hosing down everything to their front in a tremendous hail of angry red and white tracer.

They hit the bottom of the hill. Already here and there in the village the straw roofs of the *isbas* were burning. Against the lurid flames, they could see dark figures ploughing across the snow, trying to escape. The halftracks concentrated on the fleeing figures, knowing that they dare not let anyone escape. That could only bring down disaster upon them. The dark shapes fell by the score, writhing madly in the snow like puppets in the control of a suddenly demented puppet-master.

Now they were almost into the village: an armoured "V" trailing a huge wake of flying snow behind them, ignoring the enemy slugs drumming on the halftracks' metal sides like heavy tropical rain on a tin roof. Russian women soldiers, faces crazed with fear, rose up out of their foxholes. A few clutched stick grenades. The machine gunners had no mercy. They riddled them with slugs. Here and there the drivers swirled their carriers round over the foxholes, the tracks churning the snow and earth until the sides crumbled, turning the holes into horrible coffins filled with bloody pulped messes which had once been humans.

Now, while von Dodenburg directed his halftrack towards the church, others worked their way along the foxholes, full of confused, terrified Russian women who were dying like flies, helpless in the face of that armoured onslaught. The halftrack crashed through a barn, scattering hay on both sides. Directly ahead lay the onion-towered church, scarlet fire erupting from every window and crack in the stone facade. Behind, one of the halftracks reeled and came to a stop, thick smoke pouring from a suddenly ruptured engine. It was the chance the women soldiers crouching in their foxholes had been waiting for. They came out of their hiding places, howling and snarling like wild animals. Within seconds they were climbing over the sides of the stalled vehicle, hacking, slashing, cutting, carried away by the primeval animal blood lust of battle.

"Give the door a burst, gunner!" von Dodenburg yelled and ducked the next minute as a burst of enemy fire raked the inside of the halftrack.

"Frig this for a game of soldiers," Schulze yelled mightily, as next to him a trooper went down, choking in his own blood, a series of scarlet buttonholes ripped the length of his shattered chest. Schulze pulled the stick grenade from his boot and threw it with all his strength at the cupola from which the burst had come. The gold and cream structure rocked violently. The lightening conductor came tumbling down. A woman screamed shrilly and came hurtling from the parapet to hit the snow below like a wet sack of cement.

Next to von Dodenburg the driver slammed the

halftrack against the church door. It shattered and broke, hanging from its hinges. The halftrack's motor stalled. But it no longer mattered. Whooping like drunken Red Indians, the panzer grenadiers vaulted over the sides of the vehicles, firing from the hip as they belted for the sagging door. Here and there men went down, throwing up their arms, as if climbing the rungs of an invisible ladder.

Von Dodenburg dropped with the rest. He ran forward, followed by a limping Matz, snapping off shots from his automatic to left and right.

"Watch yer backs!" Schulze bellowed. He tossed a grenade over the heads of the running men. It trundled through the half-open doorway. Next moment, it exploded with a satisfying crunch. A Russian woman soldier, who had crouched there, behind one of the old fashioned machine guns with wheels that they used, came hurtling out into the snow, breasts hanging from her scorched tunic, both squirting out blood in scarlet arcs.

Von Dodenburg sprang over her writhing body and fired inside. One of the deserters came tumbling down the stone steps which led to the steeple to his right. Another came running out screaming, his face dripping down onto his chest like red molten wax, screaming, *"Nicht schiessen . . . Bitte."* Von Dodenburg shot him in the chest and he fell dying.

Now, out of the shadows, more and more of the mutineers came running towards the attackers, tears streaming down their unshaven faces, hands held high above their heads in abject surrender.

"Get rid of that rabble, Matz!" von Dodenburg yelled in disgust above the vicious snap-and-crack of the fire fight. For the Russian women were still fighting on in the gloomy smelly interior of the old church.

"You heard the officer." Matz cried, aiming a mighty kick at a laggard mutineer. "Get moving, wet tails."

"Watch it, sir," Schulze bellowed, blood trickling down the side of his face where he had been nicked. "That Russki beaver's still not finished—" He paused and fired a quick burst from his machine pistol. Plaster and stone chips rained down. A woman tumbled dead over the pulpit.

"Thanks," von Dodenburg yelled back. "I owe you one." He rushed on, ignoring the slugs which were cutting the air on all sides. For he knew speed and unrelenting attack were the only way to success in this dangerous business of house-to-house fighting. One never should allow the enemy to consolidate. He dodged behind a shattered ornate blue and gold screen and started firing upwards.

"Kuno . . . Kuno von Dodenburg," the voice came from somewhere above in the smoky gloom of the church's interior, "We've had enough. We don't want to die at the hands of our fellow countrymen."

It was Hanno von Einem. Von Dodenburg frowned. He'd have to make a decision about the traitor soon, but not now. There were other more important things to be done. "All right, you and your people come on out with your hands up."

A second later the mutineers came filing down through the line of flushed angry Wotan troopers who took out their rage on the traitors by launching kicks at them and threatening them with their weapons. Hanno von Einem appeared. He was quivering with fear. "What is going to happen to me?" he pleaded, eyes wet with tears.

Von Dodenburg didn't answer his terrified question. Instead he asked, "Where's the Russian woman, Colonel Elena Kirova?"

"She's up there with a section in the roof, Kuno," Hanno von Einem said hurriedly. "But what about—"

Von Dodenburg nodded and Matz gave the ex-officer with the scarred face a swift kick so that he staggered and nearly fell. He dismissed the traitor and snapped to Schulze, "I want no more casualties. Let's see if we can get them to surrender. Have you got any smoke, Schulze?"

The big NCO nodded.

Von Dodenburg turned to a sweating Matz, "Bring in a couple of the women."

"All right, Schulze," the officer commanded, "throw the smoke grenade."

Schulze tugged the pin and launched the grenade into space. *Crunch*! The bomb exploded. Thick smoke started to pour from it. Von Dodenburg darted forward. Too late for the women to react. As they commenced shooting, he was already in position on the other side of the nave and in the dead corner which they couldn't reach. For a few moments, he waited till the smoke cleared, then he cupped his hands about his mouth and yelled upwards. "In a minute my men will bring in some of your women as prisoners. If you do not surrender now, I *personally* will shoot one of them. If necessary I will shoot the lot. I want no more casualties. Do you understand?"

His voice rang and rang around the centre of the church. But from above came no answer. All was silence, broken only by the sounds of the flighting still going on in the village outside.

Matz came in, pushing three women in front of him. All were shaven-headed and battered, with their hands tied cruelly behind them with chicken wire. One of them, a big peasant had her shirt ripped, and from it one enormous dug bounced up and down as she staggered into the centre of the nave.

Von Dodenburg spoke again. "Get out of the way, Matz. I've got them covered." He raised his automatic, as Matz backed off into the shadows and Schulze licked his lips, as if at some fond memory, as he stared at the peasant woman's big right breast.

Von Dodenburg clicked off his safety once more. The slight click seemed enormously loud in the sudden stillness which had descended upon the nave. "I shall count to three," he said slowly, "and if you haven't surrendered by then, I shall kill the big one – the one with the torn blouse." He aimed his pistol and began to count slowly, *"One . . . two . . . th . . ."*

"All right, you German savage!" It was Colonel Kirova's voice, harsh, bitter and defeated. "We surrender."

Von Dodenburg breathed a hard-felt sigh of relief. "Throw down your weapons," he ordered, "and come on down with your hands up."

A moment later, Elena Kirova passed him, her dark eyes smouldering with hate. It was a look that Colonel von Dodenburg, as he would be by then, took with him to his grave.

Chapter Nine

They carried Hanno von Einem out to his execution at dawn. Von Dodenburg had formed his own men up in a hollow square, all of them heavily armed and facing the line of sullen mutineers. It was cold and barely light, and von Einem trembled with every limb. But it was not the cold that made him shiver so violently; it was fear, plain naked fear.

Twice, while they had tried to make him drink one last cup of "nigger sweat", as the Wotan troopers called their ersatz coffee made of acorns, he had pleaded with them not to shoot him. "What purpose will it serve? We're doomed . . . finished as it is?" He stared over Schulze's broad back, as he held the canteen cup up to the shaking man's lips, at a wooden-faced von Dodenburg. But the latter didn't respond. Von Einem had to die. There was no other way. For he was a traitor, not only to his country, but also to the officer corps, and above all to his caste. When Junkers started betraying their country, von Dodenburg knew well, then Germany was lost.

Now as they tied the shaking, moaning wretch to the post, which would hold him upright till his death, von Dodenburg had a sudden memory of Hanno and himself all those years before: naked, lithe young boys swimming in the blue-green pond behind the village, in a world which was as remote from this white hell as the moon was from the sun.

Hanno von Einem flung one last appealing look at his old school friend before they tied the blindfold on him. "Kuno –" he began and then stopped when he saw that von Dodenburg had turned his head. Tamely he resigned himself to his fate.

Hurriedly, Schulze, who was in charge of the makeshift firing squad, pinned the white heart on the condemned man's chest as a mark for the firing squad. It was a task that no one liked, but as Schulze had growled half an hour before to Matz, "It ain't every day that your hairy-assed soldier gets to shoot an officer an' gent."

Now he strode back over the fresh crisp snow to where his squad waited. A sudden hush fell over the parade. All eyes were directed at the man tied to the stake. Von Dodenburg felt himself catch his breath.

"*Present!*" Schulze barked.

The firing squad raised their rifles.

At the stake Hanno von Einem began to pray out loud, his breath fogging the air.

"*Aim!*" the firing squad squinted down the length of their rifles at the white heart pinned on the doomed man's chest.

"*FIRE!*" Schulze yelled.

There was the crash of musketry. Someone gasped. Another cried out. At the post, Hanno von Einem sagged, blood trickling out of the side of his gaping mouth and dripping onto the bright new snow. Von Dodenburg drew his pistol and, holding it down the side of his trousers like a dentist holds his forceps when he approaches a frightened child whose tooth he is going to pull, he strode to the sagging body. There was no sound now save the crunch of his boots across the snow and the steady drip-drip of the falling blood.

He paused and listened. He could hear no breathing. He pressed back von Einem's eyelid. The eyeball rolled back lifeless and unseeing. "He's dead," he announced and put away his pistol. There was no need for the *coup de grace*. "All right, Sergeant Schulze," he said with sudden formality, "cut the dead man down."

"Sir."

Von Dodenburg turned to face the line of sullen mutineers. "You've seen what has happened to your ring-leader," he announced. "The same can happen to you – all of you. What is it to be? Will you soldier on – or not?"

Some nodded. Others muttered reluctantly, "Yes." But whatever their reaction, von Dodenburg could see that they were all scared. They'd soldier on for a while, until another opportunity came along to desert. "All right," he said, "adjust your caps and your uniforms. You will arm yourselves with the weapons taken from the prisoners." He turned to One Flipper. "All right, take charge of 'em."

Von Dodenburg looked to where Schulze was cutting down the dead man. The ground was as hard as iron, so they would have to cover him with snow and that would be his grave. In the spring thaw, someone would find his bones and perhaps wonder who the dead man might have been, before passing on his way. And that would be the last of Hanno von Einem. Wild dogs would scatter the bones of the last of a family, which had fought for Prussia and Germany for over three centuries.

The thought reminded von Dodenburg that he had other duties to carry out if his bones, too, were not to rest in this village, whose very name he did not even know. He walked over to the church, now under guard of some of the re-armed deserters, strengthened by a halftrack-load of panzer grenadiers. "Are they behaving themselves?" he asked Matz who was in charge of guarding the prisoners.

"Yessir," Matz replied dutifully and then with a wink he said, "Shameful waste of all that gash, keeping 'em locked up like that."

"Go on, Matz," von Dodenburg quipped, his good mood restored now that the execution which he had quietly dreaded, was over, "they'd have you for breakfast." He opened the door and went in, assailed immediately by that well-remembered Russian smell, a compound of the black tobacco they smoked, garlic and sweat.

The women stared at him as he stood there in the door, with Matz peering in behind him, machine pistol at the ready, for he was taking no chances, women or not.

Most of the women were slumped listlessly on the floor of the nave, that fatalistic Russian peasant look on their broad faces, as if all life was simply miserable and there was nothing anyone could do about it. Some were smoking, great clumsy cigarettes of black tobacco wrapped in a newspaper sheet. A few were naked to the waist, running lighted matches around the seams of their woollen shirts in an attempt to kill the lice.

"Perhaps yer right, sir," Matz said, eyeing the half-naked women's huge pendulous breasts and muscular forearms, "I'm safer where I am."

Von Dodenburg gave a dry laugh and said, "Where's the Colonel?"

"We've put her down in the crypt thing by herself. We didn't want her stirring this little lot. They were a handful enough before. Don't want any more trouble –"

He stopped short. One of the women seeking lice had lifted up her skirt to reveal that she was naked beneath. Now she started to scratch her thick mound of pubic hair. "Christ," he commented, "she's got a beaver full of 'em as well!" He shuddered violently at the thought.

Pistol holster flap opened – just in case – von Dodenburg shoved his way through the sullen crowd of women and went down the stairs to the crypt where he, himself, had been imprisoned only hours before. He turned the key in the rusty lock and opened the heavy door. She was squatting in a pile of dirty straw, back pressed to the damp, running wall. She looked up, but her beautiful Slavic face revealed nothing when she saw who it was.

Von Dodenburg touched his hand to his battered cap. "Colonel," he said.

Again she did not react, save there seemed to be a hardening in those dark green eyes of hers.

"I have a proposition to make to you," von Dodenburg persisted.

"And I have nothing to say to you," she replied tonelessly.

"I think you will have," he answered, angry at the woman, but at the same time he could not refrain from admiring her, too. She certainly was no coward. In the face of death, she would not break down like that pathetic traitor von Einem. "If you will give me your word of honour as a Soviet officer that you will not attempt to escape, and come with us, I will set your soldiers free."

"Why do you want me?" she asked without curiosity.

"You are a reliable and valuable source of intelligence. Our people will want to know what you know."

"You will find out nothing from me about our intentions," she said stoutly, eyes flashing fire now.

"I shall leave that to our Intelligence," he said, ignoring the remark. "The alternative – for me – is to leave your women imprisoned in this church. There is no way out for them and, since the fighting last night, the peasants have fled the village. You know what that means, don't you? Your women will starve to death." He looked hard at her, awaiting her reaction.

Slowly, very slowly, she said. "You mean, you will *murder* them."

"If you like that word – yes."

"*Boshe moi*," she cursed in Russian. "What swine you Fritzes are! Murdering women in cold blood."

He shrugged with apparent carelessness. "You can't make an omelette without cracking eggs," he said. "Now, what is your answer?"

"You Germans!" she sneered. "You can't make an omelette without cracking eggs," she mimicked his words cruelly. "You always have an excuse for everything. It's not the world that is right – no, *it's* the Germans, and everyone else makes a mess of things. What neat phrases you can always think up, you Germans, for your cruelty!"

Again he felt that same stirring of his loins that he had sensed when he had first met her. It was a mixture of sexual attraction and anger at her bold defiance. The Germans were supposed to be the master race and these Slavs the slaves, as their racial name seemed to imply. But here she was – in her position – defying him, sneering at him. A sudden wave of sexual heat flushed through his body. He would dearly have loved at this very moment to strike her to the ground, rip her pants off and thrust his manhood inside her, working her to and fro with all the power of his virile young body until she was silent, or was sobbing with passion, begging for more.

She looked at him challengingly and he knew with the instant clarity of a vision that she knew what he was thinking at that very moment. He caught himself, physically restraining that almost overwhelming lust for her lips, her breasts, those thighs, that warm, wet secret place between her legs, to say coldly, "What is your answer?"

She looked at him challengingly. She ran the pink tip of her tongue between her red lips slowly, not taking her dark-green gaze off his flushed handsome face for one instant. "What can I say?" she said huskily, emphasising her words very deliberately. "I am in your power, Major von Dodenburg – *completely*." She breathed out hard. It could have been a sigh of resignation. Von Dodenburg cared to believe it wasn't . . .

Ten minutes later they were on their way, the halftracks crowded with the panzer grenadiers and the re-armed mutineers. Behind them as they left the half-destroyed village the women soldiers milled around, staring at the dead bodies of their comrades already beginning to be covered with the drifting snow, lost and wondering what they should do now that their beloved commander had been taken from them. But for Colonel Elena Kirova, they were already forgotten. All her life she had been concerned not with the past, but with the future. The handsome young German Major wanted her – physically – she knew that. Now she must turn that to her own advantage. "They must die," she told herself, as the convoy churned its way through the fresh snow, heading for the river, "*not one of the fascist pigs must escape!*" She looked down. In her fervour she had drawn blood by pressing her hands together so fiercely. She bent down and started to suck it dry, while von Dodenburg watched her and wondered . . .

Chapter Ten

"Sir . . . sir!" the signaller called excitedly over the noise of the halftrack's engine. "The Regiment's going over to the attack, sir!"

"*What?*" von Dodenburg responded immediately, as he crouched down next to the signaller whose position was just behind the driving cab in the packed vehicle. "Attack did you say?"

"Yessir. Listen – in clear, too." The excited radioman tugged off his earphones and handed them to von Dodenburg.

The latter shoved back his battered cap with its tarnished skull-and-crossbones insignia and held the phones close to his ear. Distorted and crackling, the signal, interrupted now and again by the Russian radiomen playing loud brass band recordings for exactly that purpose, read "Front crumpled . . . Karpovka . . . SS Wotan will attempt to restore . . . positions . . . repeat SS Wotan will attempt to restore –' Abruptly the voice vanished. Swiftly von Dodenburg snapped. "Try to get him back on net, Dietz."

"Sir!" Hastily the signaller began to turn his dials, while von Dodenburg pressed the earphones urgently to his ear. There were snatches of Russian. Someone cried in German, "For God's sake, let me have ari!" – the unknown speaker meant artillery fire. A woman was singing the popular song of that year, *"After every December, there's always a May."* But the Vulture's signaller stubbornly refused to turn up again on the airways. Finally the harassed signaller gave in. "Sorry, sir, I think we've lost him for the time being."

Von Dodenburg thanked him and handing him back the earphones, said, "Keep trying." He stood upright once more, narrowing his eyes against the icy wind blowing across the endless expanse of the white steppe. To their front, the horizon flickered a cherry red, and by straining his ears, he could hear the faint, muted boom of the guns from where the Russians were attempting to cross the Karpovka. To left and right in the distance, black columns of smoke were ascending to the leaden, snow-heavy sky and von Dodenburg knew what they signified. Russian reconnaissance patrols had already crossed the river and were marking their own progress to avoid being attacked by the Red Air Force. Once, too, Matz, who had the keenest eyesight of them all, thought he had spotted a group of horsemen, who might well be Cossacks.

All in all, von Dodenburg concluded, they were heading for what was the site of the enemy breakthrough into the Pocket. But why had the Vulture suddenly decided to attack when his declared intention had been to lead Wotan out of the trap of Stalingrad? Why, too, had he broadcast his intention in clear? The Russians would have picked up that signal as well, and would now be alerted to his intentions.

He looked across to where the Russian woman squatted among the panzer grenadiers, as if he might see some explanation on her pale but pretty face. But she returned his look, her features revealing nothing.

Von Dodenburg shrugged and told himself that he'd

find out what the Vulture was up to when they linked up with the rest of the Regiment. "*If!*" a harsh little voice at the back of his mind rasped.

He ignored the voice.

The column rolled on. Now the sound of gunfire grew louder, though there was no sign of any defenders. The front on the German side of the river seemed absolutely deserted. Were the Russians firing just for effect, von Dodenburg asked himself puzzled. In fact, he concluded, the whole business was bewildering. The only certainty was that the Russians were crossing the Karpovka . . .

It was an hour later that they came across the "field mattress". She came stumbling out of the firs, breasts dangling from her ripped-open blouse, her hair streaming out behind her, face contorted with fear and screaming, screaming, screaming, as if the Devil himself were behind her.

Instinctively, the driver of the first halftrack braked, as he recognized the uniform of the German Women's Auxiliary – "officers' field mattresses", as the female soldiers were called behind their backs. Hastily seizing his machine pistol, Schulze dropped over the side of the vehicle and doubled through the snow to the woman, who threw herself into his brawny arms.

"What's the matter?" Schulze demanded, as the girl seemed about to bury herself right into his chest. "Where's the fire, girl?"

But all the big NCO could get from the terrified girl was a meaningless throaty gurgling and a wild wave of her hand in the direction she had just come from. In the end, Schulze lost patience with the hysterical girl. He gave her what to him was a playful tap. But it worked. The blow across her pinched, ashen face shocked her into awareness. She sobbed, "Bodies . . . bodies . . .

everywhere . . . Cossacks!" Then she began to cry like a heartbroken child.

Schulze waved to the halftrack, pumping his free hand up and down three times, the infantry signal for advance. The panzer grenadiers took up action stations at once, as the first vehicle started to creak forward to the wood, their weapons balanced on the steel sides, faces keen and tense, ready for anything.

With von Dodenburg standing behind the cab, pistol in hand, the halftrack nosed its way through the firs carefully and then stopped. Another "field mattress" lay there sprawled out in the snow, her grey knickers ripped down about her ankles, her skinny legs spread in obscene invitation, her head a bloody mess of red gore, flecked with gleaming white chips of shattered bone, where it had been smashed in by a rifle butt. "Oh my God!" von Dodenburg breathed as his gaze went from the murdered and raped girl to the little convoy which had been overcome by the marauding Cossacks.

There were dead horses and oxen which had been pulling the carts. Now their legs were already stretched out and frozen so that they looked like tethered barrage ballons. But it wasn't the dead animals lying among the overturned and plundered carts which caught his shocked attention. It was the dead girls. All of them had been raped first. It was easy to see that, and here and there he could see the frozen blood set against their white thighs, which indicated some of the "field mattresses", as he knew troopers called them, were innocents, their virginity taken so brutally minutes before they had been done to death.

Von Dodenburg turned and looked at Elena Kirova. He could see the pain and anguish in her eyes as she viewed the terrible scene, but her jaw muscles were tensed and lips pressed tightly together, as if she were willing herself physically, and only with the greatest of effort, not to say anything. Von Dodenburg shrugged and turned to Schulze and the girl. "What happened?" he asked gently, though inwardly he raged at this outrage.

"Come on, *Fraulein*," Schulze added his voice to the C.O.'s "Tell us what you can."

The girl released herself from Schulze and then, suddenly realising that her blouse was torn and revealing her breasts, in front of all these men, she attempted to pull the material across her chest. Wordlessly the Russian woman walked over to her, took off her own coat and hung over the girl's thin shoulders. Then she walked away again.

"*Danke*," the "field mattress" breathed and huddled into the warm coat. Then she told her story. "We're a signals unit. They tried to get us out before the Pocket closed, but they couldn't . . . But everything went all right. We were twenty kilometres behind the front and in no real danger. Then the front near us along the river collapsed. Someone said the soldiers – our soldiers – had just walked out of their positions even before the Russians attacked."

"Hanno von Einem," von Dodenburg raged inwardly. He had richly deserved his death by firing squad. This terrible massacre had been caused by his treachery.

"We were told to pull out, get into the centre of the Pocket," the girl continued, her voice now oddly flat and without emotion, as if she were talking about something that had nothing to do with her. Obviously she was drifting into a state of shock. Von Dodenburg had heard men just out of combat talk like that. It was one way that they could overcome the horrors they had just experienced. "There was no transport save those peasant carts," she indicated the wrecked little panje wagons.

"But the chief – she's over there, dead like the rest – said we'd have to manage till we reached the nearest German troops. They'd look after us. We'd be all right." Suddenly she caught her breath as if she might start shrieking again hysterically. But she didn't. Instead she said, bitterness in her voice now. "They just abandoned us – to this. Ten Cossacks had me before I—"

– "You mean, German troops out here?" von Dodenburg cut in almost harshly, a sudden frightening, sickening thought beginning to unfurl in his mind.

She nodded. "With tanks," she looked directly at the young Major. "They could have taken us with them. We were German women. I know it's contrary to regulations, but we could have been saved all this."

"SS?" von Dodenburg demanded, while Schulze stared at him in growing dismay.

She nodded mutely.

"Which way did they go?"

She pointed south-west. "You can see the tracks they made. We were crying and the chief was swearing at their commander and crying at the same time. The tears were running down her face, as though she knew what was going to happen to us now they had abandoned us . . ."

Von Dodenburg was no longer listening. Instead, he stared at the broad track imprints in the snow, imprints that could have been made by no other tank than the Tiger – *the Tigers of SS Assault Regiment Wotan*! The Vulture had not been going to attack the bridgehead at all, as he had signalled. That had been a feint. He would cross farther up the river, perhaps unopposed, while the Ivans grouped for his supposed assault. He had been prepared to do everything – and anything – to save his own skin and win those general's stars of his.

Von Dodenburg was overcome with a great burning rage, such a rage that he found it almost impossible to choke out the order, "Bury them – with snow at least," he indicated the dead women.

"Can I help?" It was the Russian woman.

He nodded. He was unable to say any more.

Now she moved, together with soldiers armed with shovels, tugging down the women's skirts the best she could to hide their ravaged loins before the soldiers tossed shovelfuls of snow on their lifeless, unseeing faces. Finally the scene of the massacre was covered. Still unable to speak, von Dodenburg pointed in the direction the Tigers had taken and mouthed the word "March!"

As the halftracks started to roll once more, Schulze, taking his eyes off von Dodenburg's taut, burning face, turned to Matz and hissed, "Old house, I wouldn't like to be in the Vulture's dice-beakers when the CO catches up with him. He looks as if he's gonna have the balls off'n the Vulture – *with a blunt razor!*"

As for Elena Kirova, she told herself, "The German has a soul after all . . ."

PART THREE

Link-Up

"Heaven, arse and cloudburst – we've made it!"
Sgt Schulze to Cpl Matz, Dec. 2nd, 1942.

Chapter One

An uneasy stillness like a premonition of impending danger hung over the snowy landscape. It was so thick that the Vulture felt he could cut it with a knife. To another eye, the snow-heavy trees sparkling in the thin hard white light of a winter morning, the clean invigorating air, the immense wash of the steppe leading to the river, might have seemed beautiful: a scene of peace and winter content as portrayed by some romantic nineteenth century painter such as Spitzweg. Not to Vulture. He could smell danger as the long column of Tigers crawled towards the ford.

He knew that the Russians already had patrols on this side of the Karpovka. He had spotted one of them himself half an hour beforehand. A handful of horsemen in fur hats who had studied the metal giants through their field glasses before trotting away on their sturdy brown ponies. "Cossacks" he had informed a frightened Creeping Jesus. "But don't fear. Even the Cossacks, as brave and as dim-witted as they are, wouldn't dare tackle a Tiger." He had given Creeping Jesus a wintry smile, and added, "Nothing can stop this," he had slapped the turret of the Tiger with his gloved hand.

Now, as they came ever closer to the river, the Vulture wasn't so sure. Yet, apart from the Cossack patrol, they had seen no evidence of other Russians. Even the barrage at the spot where the enemy was preparing to cross the great river had ceased. It was as if the front had gone to sleep. Still the Vulture felt it in his bones – there was danger lurking out there somewhere. Touching his throat mike, he said, "Sunray to all. Gunners stand by. We're getting close to the ford now. *Ende.*"

The ford was clearly marked on the map, and the map itself was based on one captured from the Russians at the beginning of the drive to Stalingrad. Therefore, the Vulture told himself, it had to be accurate. According to it, the River Karpovka was just over a metre deep at this time of the year. Even accounting for extra water from melting snow, he felt the Tigers could ford it, providing the drivers didn't panic or take the river too fast creating a bow wave. All the same. The Vulture frowned and stared at the way ahead.

Now the river started to loom up ever larger. He thrust up his binoculars and surveyed first the near bank and then the other one. Nothing stirred. It was as if they were alone in a world where everyone else had died. Still the Vulture felt uneasy. He couldn't quite put his finger on it, but he felt a sense of apprehension which made the small hairs at the back of his neck stand erect.

Another half hour passed. A pale yellow winter sun had risen. Its rays sparkled thinly off the broad stretch of the river. One by one the Tigers ground to a halt, as they prepared for the crossing. Together with Creeping Jesus, the Vulture dropped from the leading Tiger and strode over the snow to the bank of the river.

Thoughtfully, the Vulture surveyed the still waters while Creeping Jesus waited impatiently, wishing that they would cross – soon. Again the Vulture raised his binoculars and searched the opposite bank; and again it was devoid of human life. He made his decision. "All right, Adjutant, we cross. You take the first Tiger across and cover us as the rest do so."

"Sir," Creeping Jesus snapped eagerly. At last they would be getting out of the damned Pocket. Once on the other side, they stood a chance of escaping the debacle to come.

Now the driver of the lead Tiger, with Creeping Jesus perched in the turret just in case it sank, started to drive it down the bank, throwing up a shower of mud and pebbles. The sixty-ton monster struck the water. The Vulture bit his bottom lip. Now they'd see if the captured Soviet map was accurate or not. Carefully the driver steered the tank with the slight current, veering a little to the right, keeping in low gear, trying to avoid a bow wave.

The water rose. It was up to the top of the smaller boogies. But as yet the exhaust pipe was above the surface of the river. Fervently the Vulture prayed that it would remain like that. Metre by metre the Tiger crossed the Karpovka, while on the bank the Wotan troopers watched, hardly daring to breathe. Then like some great metal duck, the Tiger was waddling up the opposite bank, with Creeping Jesus waving his arms wildly at the success of the crossing.

The Vulture breathed a sigh of relief. The first Tiger had done it; the rest would do the same. "Start up!" he commanded. "Five minutes' interval between each crossing. We don't want anyone to be swamped by the other chap's wake. All right pop to it!"

His crews needed no urging. They knew that troops were most vunerable crossing a river. They "popped to it".

One after another, the tanks slipped into the river, while the Vulture surveyed the scene anxiously, constantly watching his front and rear, for he simply could not throw off the brooding sense of apprehension. As he told himself, it was all too easy – too damned easy! Here they were escaping from the Pocket – and not a shot was being fired at them, after they had been spotted by the Cossack patrol. All he could conclude was that the Cossacks had not been able to report their presence because the former had not possessed a radio. But still he continued to survey the horizon for the first sign of danger.

Still, when the attack came, it caught the Vulture completely by surprise. Suddenly, startlingly, the white-clad ski troops came hissing across the snow. Behind them, the mortarmen had already set up their tubes and were covering the advance of their comrades with a swift barrage of mortar shells.

In an instant, all was panic and sudden chaos as the bombs began falling in the river, sending up huge spouts of water and threatening to stall the Tigers' motors. Frantically, the Vulture yelled above the racket, *"Return fire . . .* For *Chrissake, return their* fire, *you slow-witted idiots!"*

Creeping Jesus ducked instinctively below the cover of the turret as the gunner cranked the ten ton turret round to face up to this new challenge. But already the ski troops, little agile men with the yellow faces and slant eyes of the elite Siberian mountain divisions, were flinging off their skis and dropping into the snow, tommy guns already blazing.

Now the Vulture saw they had walked into a trap. The Russians had waited until half his force was across the Karpovka, with the rest either in the water or waiting to cross before attacking. Effectively, the enemy had reduced his strength dramatically. He knew instinctively that he would now have to stand fast and fight it out. In this kind of fight, his sixty ton tanks with their enormous 88mm guns were almost useless. What he needed was infantry and he had none.

He made his decision. "Stop the crossing!" he yelled into his throat mike. All gunners use their co-axials," he meant the turret machine guns. "Keep 'em down . . . Don't let them get moving! –" He stopped short, as one of the little Siberians, bulky and awkward in his padded white ski suit, started to run for his own tank, what looked like a bell in his gloved hand. But the Vulture knew this was no bell. The Siberian was carrying a hollow-charge sticky bomb, which he would attempt to clamp to the side of the Tiger. Once he did that, even the Tiger's thick metal hide would not stop the force of the explosion which would rip its guts out instantly.

Desperately the Vulture squeezed the trigger of his automatic. The Siberian flung up his hands. The bomb fell to the ground. An instant later it exploded in a vicous spurt of cherry-red flame. The Siberian screamed shrilly. Next moment his tortured body was ripped apart, splattering the surface of the snow with crimson gore and steaming chunks of shattered flesh. But already other Siberians were springing up from the snow and charging forward on their suicidal mission.

"Keep firing," the Vulture yelled into his mike, "and moving. Don't let the yellow apes get to your rear –" The rest of his command was drowned as one of the Siberians flung himself at one of the Tigers stationary on the bank and crushed his body against its engine cowling. The Tiger bucked like a wild horse being put to the saddle for the first time. Both tracks slammed to the ground. Thick white smoke started to pour from its ruptured Maybach engine. Of the Siberian there was no sign. His body had disintegrated in the explosion.

But now the Tigers were moving, their anxious frightened gunners firing wild bursts to left and right, trying to keep the Siberians on the ground, while the latter's mortarmen fired round after round, attempting to land a bomb inside the turret.

"*Button up . . . button up!*" the Vulture cried frantically, as he tried to counter the new threat, pulling down the hatch lid, effectively cutting off his all-round vision.

It was then that the first of the T-34's started to breast the hill to Wotan's right. They were no match for the massive Tigers, but even as he spotted them in the prism of the periscope, the Vulture knew that the enemy would throw in the Russian tanks in their score. If he couldn't pull something out of the hat, it was going to be a slogging match, with the Russians using their massive superiority in men and amour to wear Wotan down. "*Damn . . . damn . . . damn!*" he cursed, feeling, as yet another squadron of the Soviet tanks came racing over the top of the hill guns blazing already, that everything was beginning to go wrong, "Where in three devils' name is damned von Dodenburg? Where are those shitting panzer grenadiers of his – just when I can use them?" But there were no answers to those overwhelming questions. The Vulture was on his own. It appeared that Wotan was going to die at this God-forsaken place in the middle of nowhere . . .

Chapter Two

Kuno von Dodenburg looked at the Russian woman in the yellow light of the flickering candle. Outside the *isba* yet another snowstorm raged and the flame trembled all the time as the wind came through the cracks in the door of the one-roomed hut. "I'm going to release you once we leave the Pocket," he said, his mind made up. All day the Russian woman had tended the raped "field mattress" and had comforted her until she had been brought to some kind of normal state of mind. The sight of the two, the German auxiliary and the Soviet colonel with their arms around each other, as they had trailed over that endless steppe, had impressed von Dodenburg. He had realised he could not subject her to the horrors of life behind the wire once Intelligence had finished with her. He knew full well how Soviet prisoners-of-war died by their hundreds each day due to neglect and malnutrition. He couldn't let that happen to her.

She looked hard at him in the yellow light, her shadow wavering and moving on the dirty white wall behind her. "Why?" she asked simply and directly, "I am your enemy?"

He considered. "Once you were," he answered slowly, looking at her beautiful face as if he were seeing her for the very first time.

"And now?"

He shrugged. "I don't know exactly . . . You're a woman, a beautiful woman, that's all there is to it," he stuttered lamely.

Suddenly tears welled up in those dark green eyes of hers. "You ought not to speak to me like that," she said thickly.

He looked surprised. "Why, what did you think—"

– "Oh shut up," she interrupted him and wiped her eyes hastily. "You make me remember that there is another life than this," she swept her arms round almost angrily. "Something which isn't war." Abruptly she got to her feet and flung herself into his arms. "*Anything*," she panted, pressing herself against him fiercely, "anything you want . . . it's yours, Kuno."

Automatically his hands fell on her breasts, proud and strong under the thick material of her army shirt. She gasped and pressed herself ever closer to him, her nipples suddenly large and erect.

He swallowed hard. What he was doing was quite wrong. He knew that. But what did it matter? He might be dead on the morrow when they reached the river. He had been living off his nerves – and borrowed time – for years now.

Her hand fell to his knee. She ran it slowly up his thigh. His heart began to beat furiously and suddenly he seemed out of breath. She felt between his legs. He was erect in a flash. She started to unbutton his flies. He brushed her hand away and did the job himself. She cradled his stiff member in both hands, as if it was something very precious. Then she bent slowly and pressed her wet lips against it. He shivered with excitement . . .

On the stone bench that ran the length of the great stove, they lay naked under the single blanket, their bodies lathered in sweat, clasped in each other's arms.

There was no sound save the crisp stamp of the sentries' boots on the frozen snow, and the howl of the wind outside.

"Why?" she asked after a while.

"Why what?" he responded, gently stroking her splendid breast.

"Why keep on fighting?"

"There's nothing else for me."

She sat up slowly, her long blonde hair tousled and matted with the passion of their frenzied love-making. She gazed down at him, almost like a fond mother might do to a beloved child. "But there's no hope for you and your country. You have half the world ranged against you. America, the British Empire, we Soviets."

Idly he licked her left nipple with his tongue and she shivered with pleasure, before he said, "You might be right. But we of the SS have no other choice. If we don't fight, we die. If we fight, we might still have a chance of living."

She laughed softly. "You sound like one of us fatalistic Russians. *Nitchivo* and all that."

Now it was his turn to laugh, too.

They were silent then for what seemed a long time. Then slowly delicately, she pushed back the single blanket to expose his lean, hard body. Her hand slid along his stomach. "Can I excite you?" she asked in a small voice. "It will be the last time." He did not see the tears in her eyes, as his greedy hands reached up to seize her nipples.

Outside, the "field mattress", shivered with cold. Yet she could not bring herself to take her eye away from the crack in the rough wooden door. Now she saw the Russian woman straddle the officer, her head thrust back in ecstasy, meaningless sounds coming from her slack gaping mouth, as she pumped herself up and down savagely.

She was repulsed yet excited by the sight. The two of them lathered in sweat, their shadows magnified by the wildly flickering light of that single yellow candle, celebrating this crazy, frantic animal dance. Despite the cold, she felt herself flush. How could a German officer let a Russian woman, one of those Asiatic sub-humans, do that to him? It was worse than the rape which had been inflicted upon her. She would have to report it. After all it was a crime, wasn't it?

Finally the cold got too much for her. She stole back to her own *isba*, followed by that frantic laboured breathing, as if the two of them were fighting for life . . .

Four hours later, they were on their way once again, fighting the cold and the constant danger that their engines might seize up, trailing across that endless white plain that seemed devoid of any life. But they knew that wasn't the case. For they could already hear the hollow boom of cannon and the wild snap-and-crackle of a small arms fight. Schulze in the lead halftrack looked at his comrade Matz gloomily, "No mistaking that."

Matz nodded. "Yes, an 88mm. One of ours."

Schulze tugged the dewdrop off the end of his red nose and tossed it expertly over the side of the vehicle. "*Jawohl*, that puffed-up pineapple shitter, the Vulture, thought he was gonna get away. And you know what thought did, don't yer, Matzi?"

"Yer, he thought he'd shat hissen – and he had." He shrugged. "Well, I suppose we'll have to heave him out of the ordure."

Von Dodenburg, standing just in front of them peering at the way ahead, realised that the little, one-legged corporal was right. They would have to get the Vulture out of the shit.

Thirty minutes later they breasted a height and came to a sudden stop as they saw the battle which was being fought below at the river. On the nearest bank a Tiger was burning fiercely, while others were trundling back and forth firing at what looked like a squadron of Russian T-34s which had backed down to a hull-down position so that only their cannon were visible to the defenders. On the far bank, another half dozen Tigers had taken up the challenge from a group of firs. In an instant von Dodenburg saw why the Vulture had not broken off the fight and fled. Three of the giant Tigers were stalled in the middle of the river with Russian shells falling all around them, totally helpless and immobile.

Von Dodenburg made some quick decisions. He knew his halftracks couldn't tackle the T-34s. But his panzer grenadiers, armed with rocket-launchers, could. The trick was in getting his men through the ski troops, close enough to knock out the T-34s with their grenades. "All right, bale out!" he commanded.

Expertly the panzer grenadiers vaulted over the sides of the halftracks, as von Dodenburg snapped, "You take one group, Schulze. I'll take the other. At the moment we've got the surprise on them. Try to keep it that way. I don't want to lose a man more than necessary."

"Yessir," Schulze replied hastily, picking up his machine pistol as if it were a child's toy with his massive fist. He nodded to his two sections and snapped, "All right, you don't need a frigging written invite. After me."

Bent double, as if they were advancing against a high wind, well spread out, as they had been trained to do, the troopers, doubled through the ankle-deep snow, still unobserved by the Russians engaged in the fight with the Tigers.

Von Dodenburg turned to the two women. "You," he said hurriedly to the "field mattress", "stay with the driver and keep your head down." He waved her away with his hand. She flushed angrily and for a moment, it looked as if she wouldn't go. Then she moved over to the driver in the cab.

Briefly von Dodenburg touched Elena's hand. "You should go now before this—" He left the rest of the sentence unsaid. He knew she knew what he meant.

"I shall never see you again," she said flatly, her voice devoid, or so it seemed, of emotion.

He nodded.

She opened her mouth, as if to say something, thought better of it and got out of the halftrack without another word. Slowly, her pretty head bent slightly to one side, she started ploughing back the way they had come. He watched her go. After about a hundred metres, she turned and looked back at him for a moment. She didn't wave. Neither did he. Then she started walking again. A moment later she had disappeared into the trees.

Von Dodenburg stood there a few moments longer. Then he shook himself like a man trying to wake up from a heavy sleep. Already his sections were moving through the snow, weapons at the ready. Von Dodenburg doubled heavily after them, not seeing the look of bitter rage on the "field mattress's" face.

Matz came slithering out of the trees in a wake of snow. "The C.O. seems to be trying to move the Tigers on this side of the river into the water, sir," he reported. "The Popovs have stopped the move. They're coming out of their positions." He gave a jerk of his head in the direction of the Russian line. "You can hear them starting up their engines already."

Von Dodenburg nodded his understanding, telling himself that a withdrawal to the water was going to be a very tricky business for the Vulture, but it was to their advantage. The T-34s would be exposing their weakest spot to his grenadiers with their rocket launchers – their thinly armoured rumps. With a bit of luck, he might just be able to catch them by surprise and save the Vulture. "All right, you little rogue," he snapped, new hope in his voice, "Let's go and plant a few nasty fireworks up the Ivans' asses . . ."

Chapter Three

"Get a towing cable to the first one!" the Vulture shrieked over the radio. "Try to tow the thing out of the water while there's still time!"

"But," Creeping Jesus quavered, "it's dangerous."

"Get it done. *Ende!*" He peered through the periscope as the first of the T-34s came lumbering out of their hull-down positions into the attack. The Vulture made his first snap decision. Russian tanks had no radios save for the command tank. Usually the enemy tankers communicated with each other by means of small coloured flags. The command tank would be the only one with an aerial. Knock that out and it might slow the Russian attack down a little, he reasoned.

He swung the periscope round. There it was. In the weak winter sunshine, a solitary aerial whipped back and forth like a silver whip. That would be the Russian squadron leader.

"Gunner!" he yelled above the roar of the Tiger's 400HP engine, "T-34 at three o'clock. Fire at will."

The gunner in the turret next to him needed no second invitation. He thrust his eye against the rubber cap of the telescopic sight and watched as the low-slung T-34 slid into the circle of calibrated glass. When it was dissected by the crosswires, then he would fire. He waited tensely, as did the Vulture, too, knowing as he did, that time was running out for Wotan. Soon the Ivans would have dive-bombers supporting them.

The gunner started to count off the seconds. *"Three . . . two . . . one—"*

Like a blow from a gigantic fist, something slammed into the Tiger's side and rocked it back and forth on its bogies. For one horrifying moment, the inside of the turret glowed an angry pink, as the enemy's armour-piercing shell tried to pierce the Tiger's thick metal hide. The two men stared at the glow as if mesmerized, for they both knew what would happen if the shell did penetrate. It would explode into thousands of razor-sharp steel fragments which would rip the flesh off them right down to the bone. In a second they might well be both terribly mutilated, dying men.

Suddenly the glow vanished and the Vulture felt the sweat trickle down the small of his back. The shell hadn't penetrated. But it had rattled the gunner. He fired. Hastily the Vulture spun the periscope round. He caught a glimpse of the white blur which was their own armour-piercing shell. But it missed its target. Instead it felled a series of trees to the T-34's right, snapping them like matchwood. "Dammit, man!" he cried in rage, as down below in the driving compartment, the driver swung the Tiger round frantically to avoid the fire of the T-34 which had sneaked up behind him, "Can't you aim straight?"

Hastily the gunner opened the breech. The shell case clattered to the floor. The turret was suddenly full of the acrid stink of burnt explosive. Automatically he turned on the extractor and rammed home another shell at the same time. But the Soviet command tank had vanished into some trees, firing smoke as it did so.

The gunner fired. About five hundred metres away,

one of the T-34s came to an abrupt stop as if it had just run into a brick wall. Angry red sparks ran the length of its engine cowling. Flames erupted from the ruptured engine. The turret hatch was thrown open. A dark figure flung himself wildly into the snow, the back of his overalls already blue with flame. Madly he writhed in the snow, rolling back and forth, until another T-34 clattered over him, flattening him like a cardboard figure.

The death of the first T-34 seemed to inspire the Russians to concentrate all their fire on the Vulture's Tiger. Shell after shell slammed into the 60-ton tank, rocking it back and forth, while the frantic panicked driver below sought to keep the Tiger's more vulnerable rear away from the Russian gunners, swirling and turning, churning up a great flying wake of snow and mud.

"Make smoke!" the Vulture yelled to the gunner, as he pulled the trigger of the smoke dischargers on his side of the turret. A series of soft plops and the smoke bombs hurtled into the air to explode twenty metres or so in front of the Tiger, its armour now shining with the silver scars the enemy shells had gouged in it.

Thick white smoke started to rise immediately. The Vulture gave one wild last look through his periscope before the smoke obscured his vision altogether. Things were going wrong, badly wrong, he could see that. The tanker that Creeping Jesus had sent with the cable to help the first tank stranded in the river was lying in the mud, obviously badly wounded, slugs cutting the ground all about him. Russian infantry was swarming forward everywhere, covered by the bulk of the T-34s. It could be only a matter of minutes before they reached Wotan's positions. *Dammit, what was he going to do?* . . .

Two hundred metres away, the two groups of panzer grenadiers paused a moment and surveyed the desperate battle going on below, as more and more Tiger commanders fired smoke and attempted to withdraw towards the river, while on the far bank the others gave them whatever support they could.

A worried von Dodenburg knew that there was no time for fancy tactics now – Wotan's positions would be overrun in a matter of minutes. "Pin point your targets!" he yelled above the racket to the panzer grenadiers armed with rocket launchers, "and give 'em hell. The rest of you keep them covered!"

Everywhere, his young troopers dropped to the snow, raising the rocket launchers to their shoulders, while next to them the others prepared to take on the Siberian ski troops if necessary. They knew the battle was going to be decided now. Without waiting for any further orders, they pressed their trigger. There was a hiss, a spurt of flame and then the first rockets, trailing fiery red sparks behind them, were heading for the unsuspecting T-34s.

Metal struck metal with a hollow boom. Balls of angry red flame exploded against the hulls of the Russian tanks. T-34s reeled to a stop everywhere, gleaming silver holes skewered in their sides. Tracks snapped and reeled out behind the T-34s. Engines burst into flame. Almost immediately the Russian assault came to a sudden stop.

For a moment it seemed the Russian commanders were so taken by surprise that they didn't know what to do. Then someone yelled an order – the ski troops turned and in a ragged line started to charge up the slope, a deep bass *"urrah"* coming from their throats.

Not for long. At that range the Wotan troopers couldn't miss. The first line of Russians simply melted away under that tremendous fire. Men went down screaming on all sides, writhing in their death throes in the snow.

Still the next line came on doggedly. Again that deep bass *"urrah"* rang out. And again the Wotan troopers, carried away by that crazed bloodlust of battle, which allows of no mercy fired and fired, the snow all around them littered with gleaming cartridge cases, empty belts for the machine guns snaking down the slope as the spandau gunners fired at a rate of one thousand rounds a minute.

This time the Russians broke. Here and there men threw away their weapons in their haste to escape. Others jostled and elbowed those behind to get away. Some fell over the dead, and were dead themselves the next moment. And then von Dodenburg was yelling, *"Ceasefire . . . save your ammo . . . ceasefire!"*

The frenetic hammering of the machine guns gave way to single shots, then ceased altogether. A loud echoing silence followed, broken only by the moans of the wounded and the crackle of the flames in the broken tanks. Suddenly the grenadiers seemed to realize what they had done. They stared as if dumb-founded, their breath coming in hectic shallow gasps, at the slaughter down the slope: the packed ranks of the dead, laid out in neat lines, their blood already turning a hard black in the freezing air.

Von Dodenburg stood there, seemingly unable to move, his mouth open stupidly like some village yokel trying to comprehend something which was beyond his comprehension. All energy was drained from his lean body, though his brain told him urgently that he had to move. The Russians would be back.

Suddenly Schulze's coarse voice broke that great brooding silence with "Come on, Matzi. Don't stand there like a wet fart in a trance! Let's see if they've got any firewater. The Popovs allus have." Together the two hard-boiled NCOs started to plod down the slope to loot the dead Russians.

"Bring up the halftracks," von Dodenburg commanded and with his automatic at the ready, he began to walk down to the river bank, keeping his eye on the Russian wounded. The Siberians were fanatics usually. But they had obviously had enough this time. They simply lay there, their dark slant eyes revealing nothing, pain or hatred, as he strode past them to where the Vulture was standing on the turret of his battered Tiger, mopping his brow.

Von Dodenburg remembered the massacred "field mattresses" and could hardly contain his anger, but he knew this was not the time for that. He saluted and reported. The Vulture said, his relief obvious, "Thank God you turned up when you did, von Dodenburg. It was nip-and-tuck." Then he was businesslike once more. "We're in a mess here, von Dodenburg. Get your men to give a hand. They'll be back one way or another, that's for certain."

Von Dodenburg saluted once more and set about the task of getting the stranded tanks out of the water and over to the other side.

Soaked and freezing, an hour later, they were on their way once more, with von Dodenburg leading the column, knowing that they would have to find warmth and shelter before darkness fell. Soon they would hit the Soviet frontline, perhaps on the morrow. If the men were going to fight, they'd need rest and hot food. Behind them they left the dead and dying Russians – and the commander of the radio tank now busy reporting to his headquarters . . .

Chapter Four

"*The front!*" von Dodenburg announced as the lead halftrack slowed to a halt.

"I know it frigging well," Schulze said slurring his words, still half drunk from the vodka he had looted from the dead Russians. "I've been here before."

"Too many frigging times," Matz agreed, throwing his empty "flatman" over the side of the vehicle.

Von Dodenburg ignored their comments. For the last thirty minutes he had been heading for this village, two hundred metres or so up the track. It was getting dark and he thought this would be the best place to spend the night. Now another four hundred metres farther on, he could see the brown zig-zag line that ran the length of the steppe, and the flares which kept sailing into the air all the time above it, which was clearly the frontline.

"Where's our lot – the heroic defenders?" Matz growled.

"Here," a weak little voice said.

As one the three men standing in the halftrack swung round. "A couple of seconds more and you'd have had something right painful up yer crapper. We thought you were the Popovs." A man had clambered out of a hole at the side of the track, a virtual dwarf with a woman's scarf wrapped round his head, with tarnished lieutenant's stars on his shoulders. He stared at them almost angrily through thick-rimmed spectacles, a panzerfaust in his tiny hands. "Nobody told us the gentlemen of the SS," they couldn't mistake the sneer in his voice, "were coming to help us."

"Hold yer water, *Herr Lieutenant*," Schulze said, "We are in the same army, yer know. Friends, yer know."

Von Dodenburg stared down at the tiny officer in his dirty, ragged greatcoat which reached down to his ankles, and told himself that he looked nothing like the blond giants they depicted on the heroic recruiting posters back in the Reich. This was a real front swine. He looked like a notary's clerk suffering from piles and dandruff. He was probably as lousy as hell too.

"I ain't had a friend in my whole frigging life," the little officer grumbled. That's why I'm in this asshole of the world."

Von Dodenburg thought it was time to break into the conversation. The long column was in danger, strung out on the track. Once the Russian artillery observers spotted them, it wouldn't take the Popovs long to bring down a barrage onto them. "What gives?"

"Not much. Shit flying day after frigging day." Von Dodenburg took out his silver flask and flipped up the cap. "Here, have a snort. It'll cheer you up."

"Nothing'll ever cheer me up a-frigging-gain," the little officer said. He accepted the silver flask, offered by an SS major, without surprise. But then he looked like a man who would never be surprised ever again.

"Are the Popovs aggressive?"

The officer shook his head. "Not if we ain't. But they're getting ready for the last big push. They've got transport all the time after dark and you can hear them singing away in their holes, full of piss and vinegar. They always get tanked up with hooch before a big push."

Von Dodenburg nodded his agreement, liking the war-weary little lieutenant. "Is there accommodation in the village for the night for us?" he asked. "We're about beat."

"Plenty. I'm down to half a dozen cripples and a couple of kids, still wet behind the spoons. Yer, there's plenty of space for your brawny lads."

"What's the approach drill?"

"Follow the track at two minute intervals. Try to keep the noise down. I don't want the Popovs bringing down any *ari* on us. No smoke after sixteen hundred hours so that means you'll have to finish preparing yer fodder by then, and no movement after nightfall. In the village, we shoot first after dark and then ask questions."

Von Dodenburg gave the little officer a weary smile and Schulze growled. "That one eats razorblades for breakfast, I'll be bound."

The little officer looked up at him and said, "And no frigging SS heroics, *Oberscharführer*, if you please. I want to try to survive till the end of the week. I'll see you later." He touched his mittened hand to the woman's shawl around his head and popped back into his hole like a frightened mouse going to ground at the first sight of a cat.

Minutes later the first halftrack was crawling carefully into the half-ruined village, the usual collection of straw-roofed *isbas* grouped around the "House of Culture", with its murals of happy Soviet collective farm workers, and a neglected, onion-roofed orthodox church. A couple of old *Wehrmacht* men carrying French rifles, and two pimply youths, who could have been hardly more than seventeen made up the garrison it seemed. As Matz remarked contemptuously, "What a bunch o' Christmas tree soldiers. One good wet fart and the whole shitting lot o' them'd fall down in a faint!"

Schulze nodded, as the driver began to steer towards the House of Culture. "Yer can say that agen. When the Popovs attack, this lot'll take their hindlegs in their mitts and run. If this is all the *Wehrmacht*'s got left, all I can say is, sell the pig, mother, and buy me frigging well-out."

"Amen to that, old house," Matz commented somberly.

It was a sentiment with which von Dodenburg agreed. The end was near in the Pocket . . .

Now it was night. They had eaten and warmed themselves, and most of them rested in the dirty straw laid on the floor of the House of Culture. But von Dodenburg couldn't rest. His mind was still too full of what had happened to the "field mattresses". He knew it was time to make his approach to the Vulture. On the morrow, they would attack the Russian line, and then it might be too late.

He had shaved for the first time in a week. Now, dressed as formally as he could manage under the circumstances, he went out into the freezing night, with the stars shining from a deep purple sky and the frost sparkling a brilliant white, so that it appeared that the village was bathed in the light of searchlights.

The Vulture's HQ was in an *isba* close to the church. Von Dodenburg snapped to the sentry in front of the door, "All right, go and warm yourself for five minutes. I'll take full responsibility."

Surprised but grateful, the frozen sentry didn't need a second invitation. He hurried away. Von Dodenburg nodded his approval. He didn't want the men to find out what he was now going to tell the Vulture.

He knocked and entered without being asked to do so.

Creeping Jesus was standing talking, while the Vulture sat, looking bored, as if the adjutant was boring him with some trivial detail while his own mind was occupied with the problems of the morrow.

Von Dodenburg saluted and snapped briskly, keeping himself tightly under control, "Adjutant, I want you to be witness to this."

Creeping Jesus' mouth fell open stupidly. "Witness . . . witness . . . to what?" he stuttered, while the Vulture stared up at von Dodenburg, as if he were seeing him for the first time.

Von Dodenburg ignored the adjutant. Instead, he barked harshly at the Vulture, "I wish to inform you, sir, that once we reach our own lines, I am going to prefer charges against you, sir."

The Vulture took the information quite calmly. "I see," he said quietly, "and what are these charges?"

"Firstly, sir, desertion in the face of the enemy. You ordered the Regiment to withdraw without permission."

The Vulture remained unmoved. "I think you know my reasoning there, von Dodenburg," he said. "What else?"

"This, sir." Von Dodenburg felt his temper roused once again. A nerve at his right temple started to twitch. He fought to control himself, while Creeping Jesus stared at him as if he had gone completely mad. "You abandoned a convoy of female auxiliaries who were defenceless. They were all raped and murdered by marauding Cossacks."

That hit home. The Vulture sat up suddenly. His hawk-like face flushed scarlet. "What did you say?"

Von Dodenburg repeated his statement, and Creeping Jesus told himself that now, the arrogant swine with all his medals had really got himself up to his hooter in the shit. The Vulture would demote him to private for this – and the bastard deserved it.

"What proof have you got for that absurd accusation?" the Vulture cried.

"I saved one of the women. She is with us now. She will testify to what happened. My men can also prove it. They were there after the event." Von Dodenburg felt himself suddenly go icy-cold as he always did in tense situations. He was in complete command.

The Vulture considered for a moment, rubbing that monstrous beak of his nose, as he always did when he was in trouble. Then he snapped, "Adjutant, find the woman. Hear her story. At the double, man!"

Creeping Jesus fled. The Vulture waited till he had gone before saying softly, "Von Dodenburg, you're my second-in-command, you know that if I am accused of desertion in the face of the enemy, you will be implicated as well?"

"It's possible. I could say that I *had* to obey your orders." Von Dodenburg forced a wry grin. "Isn't that the case with all Germans when in trouble? 'We were only obeying orders'."

"But what profit can you have from all this?" the Vulture protested. "If I get the Regiment out, no one will charge me. In a few months I shall have my general's stars and Wotan will be yours – and good luck to you."

"You will never get those general's stars if I have anything to do with it," von Dodenburg answered coldly. "If—"

"Sir." It was Creeping Jesus, his face flushed excitedly, his mean sly eyes staring at von Dodenburg in triumph. "Can I speak to you immediately?"

"Oh yes, all right," the Vulture said impatiently.

Creeping Jesus bent, hand in front of his mouth, not

taking his gaze off a suddenly puzzled von Dodenburg for a moment, and whispered hurriedly into the Vulture's ear.

The look on the Vulture's ugly face changed perceptibly. Abruptly he sat up and screwed his monocle in more firmly. With one hand he pushed Creeping Jesus away. With the other, he struck the chair, hard. "Well, my dear von Dodenburg" he announced, "it seems you have been fornicating with an important Russian female prisoner. Tut-tut, what would our dear Reichsführer, with all his crackpot racial theories say about that? More importantly, what would Intelligence do when they heard that you let this important prisoner go . . .? Von Dodenburg, I think it's *your* turn to do some explaining, isn't it? . . ."

Chapter Five

Himmler was quite elated. He said enthusiastically, "I knew, *mein Führer*, that my SS wouldn't let me down, whatever the circumstances. Now I learn that SS Assault Regiment Wotan did not abandon its positions as thought. Instead, they are about to launch an attack on the Karpovka – perhaps they are even across?" He stopped and looked hopefully at *Generaloberst* Jodl.

Jodl, as pale-faced and cold-eyed as ever, wasn't impressed by Himmler's enthusiasm. Still, he knew he couldn't lie to Hitler, but he certainly wasn't going to let the ex-chicken farmer Himmler off the hook. "Intelligence has confirmed that a German armoured regiment has crossed the Karpovka. They defeated a Siberian rifle regiment. Now this German unit – still unidentified by the way," Jodl looked pointedly at Himmler, "is somewhere – here." He strode over to the huge wall map of Russia which covered the entire surface, "Near Rogachik, where it is believed that the enemy is about to launch another thrust into the Pocket."

Hitler listened carefully to the statement, patting his dog Blondi as he did so. By now he knew there was no way to save the Sixth German Army. Von Paulus had lost his nerve and awaited the inevitable end with almost Russian fatalism. That morning, the Field Marshal had phoned the Supreme Headquarters of the Greater

German Army to report. "Can you imagine what it is like to see soldiers fall on the dead carcass of a horse, beat open the head and swallow the brains whole?" Then he had added for the benefit of the listening staff officers, "What should I say, gentlemen, as commander-in-chief of an army, when a simple soldier comes up to me and begs *'Herr Generaloberst,* can you spare me a crust of bread'." No a man like that had given up. His army was doomed and so was he.

Hitler cleared his throat. "All that remains for us, *meine Herren,*" he said slowly, as if considering his words very carefully, "is to ensure that the demise of the Sixth Army is regarded as a heroic feat – in the Army, Germany and the world. In Stalingrad, we are talking of dead men. They are in a different world from ours. From now on, till they are either all dead or surrender, their only existence will be in the history books."

As always Hitler was long-winded, Jodl thought. He hated to come to the point quickly. But this time he had hit the nail on the head. Jodl nodded his approval, while Himmler looked puzzled, wondering where all this was leading.

"The tales we do *not* want to come out of this – I emphasize the words," Hitler continued, "historic battle, full of German courage and spirit, are those of the cowards. We already hear of officers bribing their way out of the Pocket. Or of other malingerers who shoot themselves at close range through loaves of bread, so that the surgeons can't spot any powder burns associated with self-inflicted wounds." He looked solemnly at the others. "Nor do we want to hear of those officers who will undoubtedly go over to the Soviets once they have surrendered, and will work together with them to denounce their German Fatherland. *No!*" he snapped firmly. "All that we want to hear is of heroism to the very last – the last man and the last bullet, as I signalled Stalingrad. Von Paulus and his generals have failed to keep trust. It is now up to us to create the legend; yes," he wagged his finger at them, *"create it."*

"I understand, *mein Führer*," Jodl said quickly. It was the way he thought, too. Himmler, for his part, looked puzzled.

"The hospitals for the wounded from Stalingrad will be sealed off. Anyone suspected of a self-inflicted wound will be liquidated. All letters from that place will be censored. The letters which are defeatist will never reach those to whom they are addressed. On penalty of death, no one in the Reich will be allowed to listen to the Soviet radio, once they start broadcasting the statements of the Stalingrad turncoats, which Moscow undoubtedly will." He turned to Himmler. "Now to you, *Reichsführer*."

Himmler noted the title and told himself that he had still not regained the confidence of the Führer.

"*If* and *when* SS Assault Regiment Wotan does break through the Soviet front and reaches our own lines, this is what will be done." Hitler stared hard at Himmler. "Every company commander and senior NCO will be cross-examined, if necessary by the sharpish means." Himmler knew what that formula meant, for he had invented the term himself. It meant that the suspect could be tortured. "They will be asked whether their regimental commander –" Hitler snapped his fingers angrily.

Hastily Himmler supplied the name he wanted, "Geier, *mein Führer*". "Yes, this fellow Geier. Whether Geier deserted the front without permission, or whether he genuinely attempted to bring his regiment to safety in order to continue the holy German struggle against the Red plague. Is that understood?"

"*Jawohl, mein Führer.*"

"If we discover that Geier deliberately deserted the Pocket," Hitler continued, "SS Assault Regiment Wotan will be disbanded and—"

– "But *mein Führer*," Wotan is the premier regiment of the whole of the Armed SS!" Himmler protested in alarm, his face blanched.

Hitler went on as if he had not heard Himmler's protest. "But before it is disbanded, an example must be made. Representatives from each major SS formation will be witness to a great blood-letting."

Now it was Jodl's turn to look alarmed.

"One in four officers, naturally this Geier first, will be shot. One in eight of the senior NCOs and one in sixteen of the men. That will be a message to the SS, and naturally the whole of the Armed Forces, that we will not tolerate cowardice and treachery in battle." Hitler patted Blondi without a visible sign of emotion on his pasty face. It was, as if he had just commented on the state of the weather.

"But isn't that extreme, *mein Führer*?" Jodl ventured a little cautiously.

"Back in 1917 after the Battle of Verdun, when the French Army verged on mutiny, their Marshal Petain had *whole* regiments shot. It worked. In 1918, when the German Imperial Army was faced by a similar situation, the High Command sat on their thumbs and did nothing. We all know the result. Germany was plunged into chaos and anarchy. The monarchy fell and it took Germany fifteen years to start regaining its rightful place in the world. Since 1933, I have been engaged in the holy task of making the Reich the master of Europe." Hitler looked very solemn. "Now I am sorely hurt because the heroism and sacrifice of thousands, hundreds of thousands of my brave soldiers, is nullified by a few characterless weaklings."

Hitler's eyes flashed with that old fire and fanaticism that tolerated no opposition. Voice vehement and thick with passion, he declared, "We have to create the heroic myth of Stalingrad which will be remembered over the centuries . . ." he lowered his voice significantly and stared at them – like a man demented, Jodl couldn't help thinking . . . "*even if we create that myth in blood!*"

There was a sudden hushed silence. Jodl could hear Hitler breathing harshly; otherwise no sound. He felt a cold finger of fear trace its way down the small of his back. Hitler was a madman who would stop at nothing, he knew that now.

Then Hitler said very quietly, "I think that is all for this noon, *meine Herren*." They were dismissed.

Himmler walked through the great echoing antechamber, crowded with black-uniformed flunkies and nervous ministers clutching briefcases and waiting to see the Führer, in a daze. In an hour he was scheduled to see the team of anthropologists who were trying to prove that their Allies, the Japanese, despite their yellow skin and slant eyes, were of the same race as the Aryan Germans. But he was no longer in the mood, though currently it was one of his major interests – he had already declared the Japanese to be "honorary Aryans". No, he was too preoccupied with the fate of SS Assault Regiment Wotan. *Disband Wotan! Shoot perhaps a quarter of its personnel!* God in heaven, he couldn't allow that. He had to think of something. But what . . . what in the name of three devils?

Suddenly, Bertha and *Kirsch* liquer came to his mind. That always worked. She always seemed to give him new energy, new inspiration.

Ten minutes later, after a mad dash through Berlin, with the car's siren going full blast, he stumbled into his office and cried to a startled Bertha, crouched over her typewriter, "Drop everything . . . now . . . I *need the lash!*"

Chapter Six

The whole of the Russian line quaked and trembled. From end to end, angry red light blinked like enormous blast furnaces. Hundreds of shells ripped the dawn sky apart and then there was that familiar *"hurrah"* of Russian infantry attacking.

"Now the fur, blood and snot'll begin to fly," said the little *Wehrmacht* lieutenant, who had been assigned to guard von Dodenberg – "and remember, have a loaded pistol in your hand the whole time," Creeping Jesus had snapped. Calmly he spat out his cigarette and watched, almost like a spectator at some peacetime football match, as rank after rank of Russian infantry came running over the frozen snow. "Soon the tick-tock'll really be in the pisspot."

Von Dodenburg smiled softly and nodded his agreement. The two of them squatted in the back of the Vulture's Volkswagen jeep (the Vulture and Creeping Jesus had decided they would be safer inside a Tiger. In front, there were two earnest young grenadiers with machine pistols resting on their knees. They, too, had orders to shoot if von Dodenburg made any attempt to escape during the breakout soon to come.

"You are under open arrest, von Dodenburg," the Vulture had announced after Creeping Jesus's disclosure. "I am asking you to give me your officer's word of honour not to escape." Von Dodenburg had refused angrily and thus the Creeping Jesus had ordered he would be under an armed escort until they reached German lines.

Von Dodenburg ignored the barrage and studied the Russian attack with professional interest. He knew the Ivans. They would throw in company after company with reckless bravery in the hope that they could swamp the defenders. If the first mass attack failed, they would hit the defenders with another tremendous barrage before launching yet another infantry attack. In the end, the Russians reasoned, they'd simply wear the defenders out.

But von Dodenburg knew, too, if the defenders went over to the counter-attacked after the failure of a Russian attack, it often threw the Russian commanders into a panic. Their school of tactics did not allow for defenders going over to the offensive so quickly; and Soviet commanders were wooden in their adherence to their own tactical theories.

Von Dodenburg watched as the first line of attackers went down like ninepins under German fire and said to the little officer with the glasses. "Are you thinking what I am?"

"Yes. If we stop this one, that CO of yours should order an immediate attack. We'd go through the Popovs like shit through a goose."

"Exactly. But what about your people?"

The little lieutenant took his eyes off the Soviet cavalry galloping bravely to the attack on the left flank, words flashing silver, banners streaming out straight in the breeze, and shrugged. Unless your CO mounts them on vehicles, those poor old currant-crappers o' mine don't stand a chance. Too old, too young, not mobile enough." He shrugged. "They'll die a hero's death," he smiled cynically, "for Folk, Fatherland and Führer . . sort of stuff."

Now the Russians were in full attack. Someone was sounding a bugle shrilly. Officers and noncoms yelled orders. A huge man, waving what might have been a regimental banner, cried *"Slava krasnaya armya*! An officer on a great white horse in front of the infantry thrust his sabre forward, parallel with the neck of his mount and dug his stirrups into the beast's sweat-gleaming flanks.

"This is it!" the little lieutenant yelled excitedly. "It's shit or bust now."

"Shit or bust it is!" von Dodenburg echoed, carried away by the other man's excitement.

Tracer zapped lethally between the lines. Turret machine guns joined in. It seemed as if the Russians were charging into a solid wall of steel. Still they came on. The commander on the white stallion was hit. He fell out of the saddle. Still the crazed beast galloped on, dragging him by the stirrup. On all sides, the Russians went down. Great heaps of them. Behind them, their comrades vaulted over the dead. Nothing, it seemed, could stop them now. The giant with the regimental banner fell to his knees. Before he dropped to the snow altogether, another soldier grabbed the flag. He waved it over his head, even as the tracer tore the banner to shreds, and yelled something. *"Russiya!"* the survivors yelled wildly and came on.

"Heaven arse and cloudburst!" the little officer enthused, "and our lot call them third-class sub-humans. Could you get German stubble-hoppers to do that?"

"Magnificent but not war, as someone once said," von Dodenburg commented, as the ragged lines – for now there were great gaps in their ranks everywhere – closed with the German positions around the village, their bayonets flashing as they lunged at the defenders in the foremost trenches, little tommy guns chattering at their hips.

But the steam was going out of the Russian attack. They were suffering too many casualties and they were no longer covered by their own barrage. It was the moment that the Vulture had been waiting for. "Fire one round!" he yelled through his mike, and then as the Tigers' guns boomed and the great 88mm shells tore the air apart like a giant piece of canvas being ripped, "Start up . . . Drivers will advance!" Shrieking and howling like banshees, the one hundred pound shells, packed with high explosive, descended upon the Russian infantry. Suddenly all was chaos, smoke, sudden death. Great steaming holes, like the work of giant moles, appeared in the snow, as if by magic. Men, already dead, bags of bloody, shattered limbs, fell from the air. Others dropped, limbs severed by the razor-sharp shrapnel which flew everywhere, shrieking in agony, blood splattering the snow in great scarlet gobs.

The attack faltered. The man carrying the banner went down, still trying to keep himself upright with its pole, fighting desperately to stay on his feet. To no avail! With one last despairing groan, he sank to his knees and then fell flat on his face, dead before he hit the snow. The banner tumbled from his suddenly lifeless hands.

That seemed to act as a signal. What was left of the assault regiment turned. They fled, dropping their weapons as they did. Here and there red-faced furious NCOs shrilled their whistles. Officers lashed about them with the flat of their swords. In vain. The rout had commenced.

"Shit that for a game o' soldiers!" the little officer said. "They've had it. *Here we go!*"

Now the first of the Tigers began to rumble out of the village in the direction of the Russian lines. Each was accompanied by a halftrack of panzer grenadiers, weapons at the ready. Slowly the metal monsters spread out into a great armoured V, their cannon swinging to left and right like the snouts of predatory creatures seeking their prey. The driver of their jeep thrust home first gear. He moved forward. Von Dodenburg guessed the driver wanted the cover of one of the tanks in front of him. Behind them came the rattle of a halftrack which shouldn't have been there. Von Dodenburg turned, surprised. Two well-remembered faces grinned down at him: Matz and Schulze. The racket was too loud for him to enquire what they were doing there and not behind one of the Tigers. But he knew. The two rogues were fussing over him like mother hens. They were out to protect him, come what may.

The little lieutenant saw his look as they started to roll forward and yelled, "Nice to be loved, isn't it?"

Von Dodenburg grinned.

Now the Russian anti-tank guns took up the challenge, as the Tigers rolled ever closer. Cannon thudded. Solid anti-tank shells hissed in a white blur towards the German tanks. Metal struck metal in a hollow boom. But the Tigers seemed to shrug off the Russian shells. Here and there, their thick metal hide was scarred by a shell, but the AP ammunition was failing to penetrate.

In their tight metal boxes, the Wotan gunners started to deal out punishment. The great overhanging 88mm belched fire. At that range, the gunners could hardly miss. Gun after Russian gun was knocked out, as the tanks rumbled forward, heading for the lines of the infantry.

Watching from the jeep, and followed by Schulze

and Matz in the halftrack, von Dodenburg knew the attack was now reaching the crucial stage. It was all a question of whether the Russian infantry panicked and ran or not. If they didn't, then the tanks would have the very dangerous job of winkling them out of their foxholes, risking attack by Russian rocket-launchers.

The old hares, Matz and Schulze, knew the danger, too. Balling his fists tensely, Schulze growled, "For fuck's sake, pick up yer hooves and fuckin' run, you bunch of birdbrains!"

Next to him Matz said nothing. Instead, he bit his bottom lip and watched as the lead Tiger approached the first of the Russian foxholes. A hundred metres ... fifty ... twenty-five metres and Russians still hadn't fled. Did that mean they were going to stick it out?

Suddenly, the Tiger stopped. Had it been hit? No, the driver was using the old and deadly Wotan technique for dealing with stubborn stubble-hoppers. The Tiger started to circle, crushing in the sides of the hole, filling it with lethal exhaust gas.

Matz bit his bottom lip till the blood came – unnoticed. He could well imagine the panic-stricken Popovs, crapping themselves with fear, as the earth crumbled and that deadly gas came flooding in. They were going to be buried alive. The hole would become their grave.

Suddenly the Tiger lurched, its buried left track throwing up wild spurts of earth and pebbles.

"*Himmel, Arsch und Wolkenbruch!*" Schulze cried. "He's shitting well done it!"

Matz knew what he meant. The hole had collapsed. The Russians were either dead or buried alive.

A minute later, the Tiger's driver had rolled on and

the Russians were clambering panic-stricken out of their holes and streaming to the rear, throwing away their weapons as they ran. *SS Assault Regiment Wotan was through the Russian frontline*!

Chapter Eight

It was now an hour since they had burst through the Russian line with such fury, scattering their infantry, knocking out the handful of Red Army trucks. Everywhere, the panicked Russians had tried to surrender to them. But the Vulture had had no time for prisoners. "Scatter them . . . kill them . . . but make them get out of the way!" he had yelled above the roar of the Tiger's engines and the gunner had fired bursts above the heads of the would-be prisoners. They, too, had fled across the steppe.

Now they were alone in that white waste, heading for the nearest German positions some twenty kilometres away, with every man in the open halftracks staring at the sky for the first sight of a Russian dive-bomber, praying at the same time that the leaden sky would soon unleash another snowstorm and give them the cover they needed. But the sky stayed leaden and that was all.

"The Popovs are a shade slow and their communications system isn't too hot," the little lieutenant was saying, "but they'll get on to us –" He swallowed hard and gasped, "Shit on shingle, there they are!"

Von Dodenburg swung round swiftly and stared in the same direction as the *Wehrmacht* officer. A fleet of small tracked vehicles was hurrying across the steppe towards them, churning up a wild, white wake of snow. Von

Dodenburg flung up his glasses. The first one flashed into his binoculars. It was a squat, little mini-tank, towing behind it a trailer which bounced and juddered up and down. But it was not the trailer which caught von Dodenburg's attention. It was the strange, ugly cannon in the centre of the open tank and the two men standing over it. Both seemed to be masked and wearing goggles.

Swiftly he handed the glasses to his neighbour. "Have a look," he ordered, "what do you make of them?"

The little lieutenant thrust his spectacles onto his forehead and peered hastily through the binoculars. "Holy shitting strawsack," he groaned, the next instant, "not those bastards!"

"What bastards . . . What are they?" von Dodenburg queried hurriedly, noting the little officer's face had suddenly turned ashen.

"I've only seen 'em once before and I told myself then, before we did a bunk, I never want to see the devilish things again."

"But what *are* they?"

The little lieutenant lowered his glasses. "Flame-throwers," he answered simply.

Von Dodenburg gasped and up in the driving seat, the driver was shocked enough to take his hands off the wheel for a moment before he recovered himself. For, even the hardened old hares of Wotan feared flame-throwers. As for von Dodenburg, a nightmarish vision of his childhood flashed in front of his mind's eye – *Generaloberst* Hammerschmitt slowly unwrapping the black bandage he always wore around his head, to reveal a ghastly, scarred, bald head, scarlet and pitted like that of some Egyptian mummy. Where the ears had once been, there were two dark holes, oozing yellow wax. "Flame-thrower," the old general had said,

"Caught by a flame-thrower back in Sixteen at Verdun, my boy."

His father had comforted him afterwards, when he had run screaming from the study, hung with tattered banners and momentoes of three hundred years of service to the Prussian crown. But he had slept badly thereafter. Now, it seemed, he was going to have to face up to that terrible weapon which had mutilated the old general.

The little lieutenant seemed to have been able to read his thoughts, for he said, "They're absolutely crap-pots to hit. They're so fast and nippy. Their only defect is that they'll have to get within a hundred metres or so to be effective. Oh, my God!"

There was a sudden hush of air. A forked tongue of oil-flecked, scarlet flame shot out a hundred metres to the front of the leading vehicle. In an instant, the snow to its fore melted, leaving behind a dark streak of discoloured earth. Even at that distance, the men in the open Volkswagen jeep could feel the searing heat. It took their breath away.

Von Dodenberg wiped the sudden sweat off his brow and gasped. The men in the leading halftrack had obviously panicked at the sight of that all-consuming tongue of flame. They had ducked behind the cover of the steel sides. Now von Dodenburg cried, "Stand up . . . fight them off. *Keep firing!*"

Already it was too late. Again that terrible rod of flame thrust out, steaming and shrieking like a live thing. It engulfed the halftrack. Its sides glowed an angry pink. In an instant, the fuel tanks went up. A terrible flame seared the length of the halftrack like a giant blowtorch. Men fell screaming into the melting, steaming snow, horrible charred dwarves who were dead or dying in agony before they hit the ground. One moment later, the halftrack disintegrated, metal flying through the air everywhere.

Now the Tigers began to react. Their great guns boomed. Scarlet flame spat from their muzzles. Abruptly, the air was full of the thwock and grunt of shells being fired. But the little armoured vehicles were incredibly swift and agile, twisting and turning as their drivers spun their wheels to left and right. Time and time again, it seemed that one or other of them would be hit, but always the fearsome little machines came through unscathed.

Then at last, Wotan struck lucky. A great one hundred pound shell slammed into the leading flame-thrower. The vehicle was thrown on its left side, tracks whirling helplessly. Probably the gunner had slumped dead over his weapon, hand on the trigger. A fatal mistake.

The terrible weapon jetted flame. It engulfed two of the others zig-zagging wildly to keep out of the range of the Tigers' cannons. In an instant all was chaos. Immediately the two fuel tanks towed on the trailers went up. The blast was tremendous. Von Dodenburg felt the air being torn out of his lungs; he coughed and choked, as if he were being strangled. Two huge sheets of flame raced skywards, as the two vehicles burned fiercely, melting the snow all around them, blackening the earth beneath.

It was too much for the rest. As if in obedience to some unspoken command, they turned tail and scurried away, back the way they had come, followed by Wotan's shells. Minutes later, they were just black dots on that infinite white waste.

The little officer took off his glasses and wiped the sweat from his high forehead with a dirty handkerchief. "Phew!" he gasped, "that's the warmest I've been in a month of Sundays here in Popovland. But

I could do without that kind of heating. By Christ, I can!"

Von Dodenburg said nothing for a moment. He was thinking hard. Over by the burning halftrack, another one had braked and the panzer grenadiers were standing in the melting snow, looking a little helplessly at the charred, burning corpses of their comrades.

The attack by the flame-throwers told von Dodenburg that they were now probably in for trouble all the way to the German lines. The Russians wouldn't give up. Admittedly, they'd know that the Tigers were virtually impregnable. They, the Russians, did not have a tank that could match the Tiger. But there was still their air force. The Russian *stormovik* dive-bomber, carrying a couple of 250 pound bombs, could certainly knock out the Tiger. Almost unconsciously, he looked up at the grey, leaden sky.

The little lieutenant followed the direction of his gaze and said, "You thinking what I am?"

"Yes."

The little officer forced a grin. "Well, let's start praying for snow!"

The flame thrower attack had badly shaken the Vulture. He reasoned, like von Dodenburg, that he now faced constant attack until he reached the Manstein army. Whatever happened, he knew he was going to take casualties. There was no chance of his bringing out the bulk of Wotan; and if he couldn't do that, he would not be able to defend his withdrawal without orders. Suddenly, he saw those coveted general's stars vanishing for ever. He had to do something to cover himself *now*!

He made up his mind. "Listen, Adjutant," he said urgently to Creeping Jesus. "I want you to send a signal over the command radio. We're going to break radio silence and signal *Reichsführer* Himmler personally."

Creeping Jesus looked suitably impressed. The Vulture was jumping the chain of command altogether. "What is the signal, sir?"

"Request fighter cover. Attempting to fight off superior enemy forces. Urgent. *WOTAN*."

Swiftly Creeping Jesus wrote down the message. When he was finished, the Vulture snapped, "You see what I'm doing? I'm telling the High Command that we're attacking, *not* running away. Whatever happens now, we'll be in the clear."

Creeping Jesus positively beamed. "I see, sir. Yessir, I see." Hurriedly he started to encode the signal, while the Vulture stared at the patch of sky that he could see through the turret hatch. But he stared in vain. It stubbornly refused to snow . . .

Chapter Nine

"*Even God won't piss on us now!*" Schulze lamented as he stared at the sky. "When yer don't want it, it pours down the white stuff all the shitting time. Now, when we do – *nix!*" He spat angrily over the side of the halftrack.

"It'll come, Schulzi," Matz tried to appease him. "That sky's full of violins," he said, using the soldier's expression for snow.

"Yer, but when? As you know, even a birdbrain like you, we're in for a right bashing. Soon. And I don't want it. If it snows, we can take off – the CO with us. We're not going to leave him with that hook-nosed, warm brother," he meant the homosexual Vulture "and his girl friend, Creeping Jesus."

Matz looked astonished. "Do you mean that Creeping Jesus is one of them as well." He made a limp wrist.

"Course not, arse-with-ears. Creeping Jesus ain't even got one in the first place. Ain't yer ever noticed what hairy palms he's got from playing with the five-fingered widow?" He laughed hollowly and nodded at the "field mattress" riding up front in the cab next to the driver, "and she's gonna get her knickers taken down as well!"

Matz made the sign of the cross over Schulze's mighty chest and intoned, "God be with you, my children. May He make your loins fruitful and your vessels overflow with goodness."

Schulze thrust up a middle finger like a hairy pork sausage.

Matz shook his head. "Can't. Already got a double-decker Berlin bus up there, old house."

"Ner," Schulze explained. "I wouldn't want to do the double-backed beast with her, even if she was the last bit o' gash in the world. I just want her to get lost – *on purpose*." He winked knowingly. "Then, what kind of evidence has the Vulture got against the CO." He glanced over to the Volkswagen jeep, reassuring himself seemingly that von Dodenburg was still there.

"What do we do then?" Matz asked.

"We get lost in the great retreat." With a nod he indicated the boom of the guns coming from inside the Pocket. "We're on the run in Russia, Matzi, and the shitting Popovs are never gonna let us stop again till we get back to the Reich. It's gonna be shit-order and shambles from here on in. Nobody's gonna take any account of a handful of SS men, no sir!"

"I suppose you're right," Matz said a little reluctantly.

"Course I'm right. Frau Schulze's handsome son is *allus* right." He forced a smile. "And yer know what retreats are like, Matzi? Plenty o' classy fodder like what the officers and gents get. Lots of lovely beaver with the dames of the rear echelon stallions. And – if we're frigging lucky with it – we won't end up looking at taties from below."

"Amen to that, Schulzi," Matz said brightening up considerably. Then his wizened face fell once more. "Ar, but there's a catch."

"What?"

"*Where's the frigging snow . . . ?*"

The Great Man sat brooding on the throne like chair at

193

the end of the great marble hall. Opposite him on a dais was the tomb of his long dead wife, at which he gazed like a figure in some 18th century classical painting. But then, despite his enormous girth and definitely unclassical figure, there was something of the Roman about the *Reichsmarschall*. For at the moment – he changed his clothes perhaps ten times a day – he was dressed in a toga-like, green hunting dress, his fat fingers, with their painted nails and heavy gold rings, clutching a hunting knife like the short stabbing sword of a Roman centurion. At his feet there was a lion cub. Its name was "Ceasar".

He took no notice of the hollow footsteps echoing down the great hall as the giant adjutant approached with the SS officer, dressed in pre-war black uniform, medals ranged in a glittering silver across his breast. As always when he had sniffed his morning dose of cocain, the huge man sank into a fit of despair and longing for the woman who had died so long before.

"*Herr Reichsmarschall!*"

Slowly, very slowly, Reichsmarshall Hermann Goering, Head of the German *Luftwaffe*, turned his head, as if it were taking his drug-crazed brain a long time to become aware of where the voice was coming from.

He stared blankly at the giant Air Force adjutant in his immaculate uniform. He held his pudgy forefinger and sucked at the great green ring which adorned it, with his painted lips. Finally his eyes came into focus and he said, "Yes?"

"*Obersturmbannführer* Zander," the adjutant barked, as if he were back on the parade ground, his voice echoing and re-echoing in that great marble hall.

"Yes?"

"*Herr Reichsmarschall,* the gentleman from the SS

has a personal message to you from *Reichsführer* SS Himmler."

For the first time, something akin to animation crossed Goering's powdered face. "Himmler," he echoed, and there was no mistaking the anger in his voice. *"Himmler."*

"Jawohl, Herr Reichsmarschall," Zander stepped in quickly.

Goering looked at the SS officer in bewilderment and distaste. "What is it, Xander?" he asked finally.

"Herr Reichsmarschall, I am the *Reichsführer's* personal representative at the High Command. Herr Himmler has asked me to make a request to you – for immediate action," Zander added quickly, knowing that this bloated monster with his drugged, painted face, only half understood what he was saying.

"What request?"

"Air support. As the head of the *Luftwaffe*—"

"Stop!" Goering said imperiously, holding up his pudgy hand at the word "air force". "I cannot make decisions about military matters without a uniform." He clicked his fingers. "A uniform – *quick*!"

Zander's mouth dropped open in amazement, but the adjutant took it in his stride. He was used to his master's moods.

"A uniform – quick. There is no time to be lost. I am in fighting mood."

Now things happened swiftly. A great bear robe was produced. Flunkies stripped the Marshal to his silken underwear, his great paunch supported by skinny white legs mottled black and blue with years of having drugs injected into their veins. Servants appeared, as if from nowhere, bearing uniforms over their arms, all elegant and designed personally by Goering. Each in his turn presented the uniform for Goering's inspection.

A splendid white velvet one was dismissed with, "No, white is the colour of innocence. There is no time for innocence now. We are fighting a total war."

"Green, no, green is the colour of hope. That will not do at all."

A black uniform was received with a shudder and a pointed glance at Zander's own black SS uniform. Zander felt himself flush. The fat madman was insulting the SS.

Finally a purple uniform was produced and Goering seized upon it with delight. "Yes, yes, purple it must be, *meine Herren*! Am I not the heir to our beloved Führer? In that colour I can safely make the same kind of decision he would make. Hurry . . . hurry," he clapped his pudgy hands like a petulant woman, "dress me."

Hurriedly the servants and flunkies started to dress him, pinning medal after medal onto his enormous chest, so that Zander felt he would have to narrow his eyes against the glare they gave off in the bright overhead lights. Finally, he was dressed and seated back on his thronelike chair, gripping his bejewelled marshal's baton in his hand. "Now," he said grandly, "you may state your wish, *Obersturmbannführer*."

"Imperial Marshal," Zander said, suddenly feeling embarrassed by the title and this whole foolishness. How could a man such as this be regarded as Hitler's successor? "*Reichsführer* SS Himmler requests you to order immediate fighter cover for one of our SS regiments attacking out of the Stalingrad Pocket. The regiment has no air cover whatsoever and is highly vulnerable, sir." He stopped lamely and waited.

It seemed an age before Goering finally spoke. He said ponderously. "Do you realise, *Obersturmbannführer*, that my *Luftwaffe* is stretched to the very limit, trying to keep the Pocket supplied? Daily, scores of my brave boys are dying, running into Stalingrad. Where am I to find the resources to save one lone regiment of the SS?"

Desperately, Zander tried another tack. "But, sir, those are transport planes. We are talking of *fighter planes*!"

Goering didn't seem to hear. "The sacrifices of my brave pilots and crews will go down in the history of the German Armed Forces." His eyes filled with tears at the thought. "And they are laying down their lives daily, nay hourly, to help others." He dabbed his wet eyes with a great florid silk handkerchief.

"But, sir –" Zander began. However, the giant adjutant shook his head and silently mouthed the words, "No use . . . he's made his mind up." Glumly Zander saluted and marched out. Goering didn't notice. He remained seated, babbling about his brave boys for what seemed an age, how they had fought unrewarded ever since September 1939, trying to fight on three fronts with antiquated machines and not enough petrol against three of the most powerful air forces in the world. But did the Führer care? Of course not. He actually blamed the *Luftwaffe* for its failure to supply the Pocket . . .

Listening to the fat marshal's ramblings, self-pitying and full of pathos, the adjutant wondered yet again if he should not volunteer for the front. It was too much for a normal man to stand – the drugs, the make-up, the wasted hours spent here in this mausoleum brooding over a woman who had been dead for nearly a decade.

Suddenly Goering stopped his rambling. He looked the adjutant straight in the face, his own fat features abruptly sly and cunning. "Well, von Bulow," he said, "we saw him off all right, didn't we, eh?"

"Yes . . . yessir," the adjutant stuttered, taken completely by surprise.

Goering gave the adjutant a crooked smile. "Now let that damned jumped-up chicken farmer, Himmler, with all that absurd Aryan nonsense of his, get out of this one by himself. See what the Führer will say when he makes a complete mess of it. Then the Führer will realise what he's got in his own loyal Goering," he tapped his fat chest with his be-ringed hand. "Yes, he'll know then who he can rely on, eh?"

"Yes," the adjutant breathed, telling himself that Germany's leaders were not just fighting the enemy; *they were fighting each other*! Now a bunch of unknown SS stubble-hoppers were going to get the chop because of it. *Crazy!*

Chapter Ten

The Stormovik came in at tree-top height. It came hurtling towards the Wotan convoy, weaving from side to side, the thin winter sun glittering on its long canopy. The lone Soviet dive-bomber caught the troopers completely off guard. They had been searching the heavens knowing that bombers needed height to drop their bombs safely. This one was a mere twenty metres above the steppe.

Wild firing broke out as the turret gunners swung their co-axial machine guns down to meet the surprise challenge. Too late! Cannon thudded the length of the plane's wings. Angry scarlet flashes erupted. White, glowing cannon shells hissed towards the Tigers.

In the lead, the Vulture screamed shrilly, as a piece of red-hot, glowing 20mm cannon shell smashed into his shoulder. Next moment he reeled forward, slumping over the gunner, whose head had vanished so surprisingly, screaming in pain. Next to him in the wrecked turret, Creeping Jesus started to scream high and hysterical like a frightened woman.

In a tight turn, the Russian plane started to climb once more. But already others were skimming over the steppe, so low that their prop-wash drew up the snow in a white fog. Again they swayed from side to side – sometimes as much as twenty or thirty metres – as the Tigers opened up with their machine guns, sending up a vicious stream of red and white tracers at the attackers.

A Stormovik was hit. Black oil spurted out and covered the canopy. Desperately, the pilot rolled over onto his back. The oil cleared. But he was too low. An instant later, he struck the ground. The plane cartwheeled once, twice, three times. Next moment, it disintegrated in a great grinding crash of rending metal. But the others came in. Soon they would be in cannon-firing distance.

Von Dodenburg groaned. There was no hope for them now. They didn't stand a chance once the Stormoviks got inside firing distance. Then it happened – suddenly . . . startlingly. The heavens opened up. In a flash visibility was down to nil and the snow was streaming from the sky as if it would never stop again.

Hoarsely, the troopers cheered as the enemy dive-bombers disappeared immediately into the whirling fog of a blizzard. For a few minutes, they could hear the roar of the engines as they tried to find a gap in the white-out. But in the end they gave up, and on the ground, the hard-pressed, weary Wotan men knew that they were safe, at least for a little while.

Von Dodenburg breathed out a sigh of relief as the planes flew away, in the same moment that Schulze and Matz came fighting their way through the raging snowstorm, big grins over their red, wet unshaven faces. One of the guards in the front of the Volkswagen jeep raised his machine pistol in warning, but Schulze growled, "Now sonny boy, don't get any fancy ideas with that popgun of yourn or I'll ram it so far up yer Keester that yer glass orbs'll pop out!" That terrible threat did it. The boy lowered his weapon hastily.

Schulze turned to von Dodenburg, "Sir," he yelled against the howl of the wind, "this is our chance. Let's do a bunk! With luck we could reach our own lines before nightfall."

Von Dodenburg bit his bottom lip. He knew that if he stayed with the Wotan, the Vulture and Creeping Jesus would not hesitate to have him court-martialled once they reached their own lines. But just to go like that – he didn't know.

"Let's not waste time, sir!" Schulze cried, the wind whipping his tattered uniform about his massive body, the snow coming down in a solid sheet. "We're all with you in the halftrack. We'll see you through."

"I know, I know," von Dodenburg yelled back a little helplessly, his handsome face contorted with indecision. "But—"

– "Von Dodenburg," a hysterical voice cut into his words. "You must take over! For God's sake take charge while we've still got a chance . . . *please*!"

Von Dodenburg swung round. Next to him, the little lieutenant exclaimed, "What in three devils' name!"

It was Creeping Jesus, his face as white as a sheet, blood dripping from his hands, as he staggered out of the white-out, mumbling and crying. At once, von Dodenburg saw that there was something wrong, seriously wrong. "What happened?" he rapped. "*Was ist los*?" Creeping Jesus' ashen face trembled violently, as if he would break down altogether in a moment and begin to sob like a frightened child.

Von Dodenburg raised his hand. Hastily, he slapped the other officer across the face – hard – and commanded, "Now then, stop that! Pull yourself together. What is it?"

Creeping Jesus shook his head and quavered. "We were hit. The CO is badly injured . . . unconscious. You must take over, von Dodenburg . . . get us out of this mess . . . while there's still time . . ." He began to cry.

"Take no frigging notice of him, sir," Schulze urged roughly. "That shit-heel wouldn't raise a frigging pinkie to help you. Why should you haul him out of the shit now?"

Von Dodenburg wasn't listening. He was thinking hard. It was a question of the Regiment or himself. What was he to do? His mind raced as the others stared at him, a tall, gaunt figure standing in the whirling snowflakes.

"All right," he snapped, his mind made up. "I lead."

"But sir—" Schulze began to object.

Von Dodenburg silenced the big NCO with a harsh, "No buts. Let's waste no more time. *Roll 'em*! . . ."

It was a strange day, full of sudden alarms and frights. Twice they heard the drone of aircraft above the long, strung-out column, obviously searching for them. For the planes dropped flares which came floating down, spluttering angrily and casting their harsh, red light on the white wall of snow. Once, close by, they heard shouts and there was the patter of machine gun slugs against their vehicles. A patrol of Cossacks loomed up suddenly out of the storm. They didn't live long.

A village loomed up in the middle of nowhere. They went through it, every gun blazing, and didn't lose a single vehicle. They came to a small stream not marked on their maps. Warily the first vehicle started to cross its frozen surface. The ice creaked and groaned alarmingly under the halftrack's weight, but it held. One by one, with von Dodenburg watching in a cold sweat, they crossed, with the ice creaking ever more alarmingly, until finally, just as the last halftrack reached the opposite bank, it cracked altogether and the water came flooding up in an angry white wave. As Schulze gasped, "Great crap on the Christmas Tree, I nearly creamed my drawers that time!" It was a sentiment with which von Dodenburg heartily agreed.

As night fell, it was still snowing as if it would never stop again. Now von Dodenburg calculated that they were some four kilometres from the Russian main frontline, facing von Manstein's German Army. Soon Wotan would be running into the Russian support positions, dumps, stores, headquarters and the like. But he hoped that the snow and the darkness would help the Regiment to break through without any great losses. Boldness and surprise would have to be the order of the day, he told himself. What had the great Napoleon always mainted – *audace, audace, toujours l'audace*! It was then that completely out of the blue, he had the idea which was to save SS Assault Regiment Wotan, not only from the Russians but also from the Gestapo. When he told the little lieutenant his intentions, the latter's weary, frozen face lit up, then fell almost immediately thereafter. "But how are you going to find the HQ?" he asked.

"You know the state of the Popov communications," von Dodenburg answered. "We've got radios everywhere. They rely on runners, little flags and that sort of thing. It's only their divisional HQs which have radios to receive orders – they say from Stalin personally. Find a command post with radio masts and the like, and you've got their HQ. Knock out their HQ, and a whole section of their line is thrown into confusion, because the Popovs will never act on their own initiative; if they get it wrong, it's either the firing squad for them or the Gulag."

"You're damned right," the other man agreed with renewed enthusiasm. "What are we waiting for?"

When the CO's order was passed to Schulze, he said, "It's gonna be hard, Matzi, old house. But if we can pull this one off, I think we'll get our dicks out of the wringer at frigging last!"

Chapter Eleven

Even above the howl of the raging wind, they could hear the rusty bedsprings and the hectic gasping of a woman. "Well, I'll be damned," Schulze whispered, "listen to them bedsprings. Some lucky arsehole is going at them pearly gates like a Yiddish fiddler's elbow. Wish I was in his place."

Von Dodenburg nudged him sharply. "All right, Casanova keep your mind off that kind of piggery and keep yer eyes peeled for sentries."

"Like a tin of skinned tomatoes," Schulze gave him back the standard answer, and wiped the driving snow from his red face.

They had located the Soviet headquarters an hour after darkness. It hadn't been particularly well blacked-out and the hum of generators had been louder than the wind. Now the row of workers' cottages which housed the staff was surrounded, with guards already posted at the Russian motor pool to prevent anyone making a break for it when they started their attack. Not that von Dodenburg wanted a noisy fire-fight which might alert the infantry who were all around in the darkness. As he had told the raiding party, "Nobble 'em with your side arms and clubs. Fire only at the last resort, when your own life is in danger."

Now they stole down the village street like thieves

in the night, some of them armed with socks filled with earth, others carrying pick handles, all of them peering through the blizzard for the first sight of the Russian HQ.

They neared the centre of the street. They passed a larger house – perhaps it had once belonged to the manager of the nearby *kolhoz* – from which came the hum of radios and the clatter of typewriters. "HQ communications," von Dodenburg whispered to the little lieutenant, who had volunteered to come with the raiding party. "We've got the right place, then."

"Yes," the other man answered, "but what do you make of that – up there?"

Von Dodenburg looked. A shaft of yellow light had cut into the blizzard. A door had been opened, from which steam now issued, thick and in a cloud rolling into the snowflakes. It was followed a moment later by a totally naked, fat man, who whooped and flung himself into the snow, turning and thrashing in it, as if he were enjoying a bathe in a very hot sea, the steam gushing up from his fat body.

"Hell's teeth," Schulze gasped. "The Popov's not got all his cups in his cupboard! Naked in this weather!"

"No," von Dodenburg corrected him, his mind racing, "he's just come out of the sauna. Now he's cooling off. Look." Another naked figure came stumbling out of the door, apparently beating himself with a bunch of twigs. He, too, flung himself into the deep snow.

Matz hissed, "They must be shitting drunk. In this weather, running around like that – stark-bollock naked! Freeze up my waterworks just looking at it. *Meschugge!*" He shook his head almost sadly at the strange sight.

Von Dodenburg wasted no more time. "It must be

them," he whispered. "Only the big shots would have a sauna like that so close to the front. Let's get 'em! *Los*!"

The two fat men lying naked in the snow, thrashing about and grunting with pleasure, stopped abruptly when they saw the German uniforms. "*Boshe moi*—" one began before Schulze kicked him cruelly with his heavy boot. He stopped abruptly, out like a light. The other one's hands shot up in surrender.

They burst into the boiling hot, steam-filled room. It presented a fantastic sight. Fat, naked men were everywhere, dousing themselves with pails of water in between taking great slugs from litre bottles of vodka, and grunting with pleasure. But there were not only men. There were naked women too: great, heavy-breasted wenches, with huge tufts of black hairs protruding from their armpits and on the base of their stomachs as they, too, doused themselves with cold water, and swallowed gulps of vodka, laughing hysterically, as they sat and squatted there in open invitation for anyone to take them – which some of the more sober Russians were already doing.

Schulze skidded to a stop at the sight, eyes bulging from his head. "Great balls of fire," he exploded, "a knocking shop on fire . . . and look at all that free gash!" He licked his lips greedily.

"Keep it down to a dull roar," von Dodenburg commanded urgently, as the naked, drunken Russians turned to stare at the intruders, as if they couldn't believe the evidence of their own eyes.

Von Dodenburg jerked up the muzzle of his automatic threateningly. "*Ruki verkh*!" he snarled.

Slowly, reluctantly, unbelievingly the Russians started to raise their hands. On the benches, the ones copulating stopped their labours and, peering through the clouds of rising steam, tried to make out what was going on. Schulze raised a fist like a small steam shovel and snapped, "*Ponenayu?*"

"*Nmentski*," they cried. "Germans!"

A great bear of a man thrust the woman who was astride him to one side and rose from the stone bench. He exuded power, sheer naked power. He scowled at the intruders, massive fists clenched angrily, his erection still protruding from his loins like a policeman's club. "What you do here, Fritzes?" he demanded in broken but understandable German. "You die – soon. Speak quick Fritzes."

Von Dodenburg stared hard at the hairy bear of a Russian. This was no mere staff officer, he told himself. This was a person of some importance, perhaps a divisonal commander. "What's your name and rank?" he asked.

Scornfully, the Russian spat on the floor. He was obviously not one bit afraid. "I tell you. Then you understand, you die," he declared, standing very erect and proud, despite his erection, "Ivan Ilyich Lyudnikov, Lieutenant-General, General Commander 3rd Russian Front."

Von Dodenburg whistled softly. They'd captured an army commander! Even Schulze was impressed. "Christ on a crutch," he said to no one in particular, "we've got a general, and he's got a horn on."

But von Dodenburg wasn't listening to Schulze. He was telling himself that they had nabbed an army commander. Whatever else happened now, the survivors would get through it with a clean bill of health. It wasn't every day that a German regiment, even one that had done a bunk from the front without orders, brought in an enemy army commander. "*Davoi*," he snapped happily in Russian. "Get your clothes on. You're coming with us."

The General looked as if he were about to protest. He changed his mind after Schulze gave his erection a light tap – well, light for Schulze – with his pick handle. Thereafter, he came quietly. Half an hour later, they were on their way again, leaving behind them a completely disrupted Soviet Army . . .

Thus it was that the remains of SS Assault Regiment Wotan started to roll through the German lines at ten o'clock on the morning of Tuesday December 2nd, 1942, a collection of rusty, shell-pocked tanks and halftracks packed with frozen, starved panzer grenadiers and the wounded, including an unconscious Vulture. The defending infantry stared up at them from their holes and trenches as if they were creatures from another world: the handful who had escaped from doomed Stalingrad.

Hastily, bottles of schnaps were passed up to them, cigarettes, chunks of black bread, slices of hard Westphalian sausage. Someone cheered. Others said, "You've done it, mates, back to mother."

Von Dodenburg took a hearty swig from a proferred flatman and felt the fiery schnaps go to his head immediately. He grinned a little foolishly. He looked around him. His men looked like ragged scarecrows. He took another swig and looked at himself, knowing that he had not shaved or washed for the last forty-eight hours. He was just as dirty and ragged. But he'd done it. He'd gotten the Regiment – what was left of it – through – and they did have their important prisoner.

He looked across at Schulze and Matz. The former was swigging schnaps, his adam's apple going up and down like an express lift, as if he would never stop. Next to him, Matz had his hand high up the skirt of one of the Russian women prisoners, his face very red. "The rogues!" he told himself, a little drunk now. "But the best rogues in all the world – the whole drunken, starved bunch of them."

With a sudden warm glow of pride, he roared above the cheers and cries of the infantry, "Soldiers, comrades – the song of Wotan!"

As one, the troopers burst into that proud hoarse chant that had accompanied them, and all of those arrogant blond giants who had gone before them, across the battlefields of half of Europe.

"Sound the trumpet
Beat the drum
Clear the street
For the men of WO-TAN . . ."

Watching them go by in their battered rusting vehicles, the infantry battalion commander shook his head in puzzled despair and admiration. He turned to his company commanders and said, "The SS, *meine Herren* . . . *the shitting brave* SS . . ."

"W-O-T-A-N" . . . it seemed to go on for ever.